INCENTIVE

PAM GODWIN

Cover Designer: Pam Godwin

Visit my website at pamgodwin.com

Disclaimer

CHAPTER 1

Decker

"You look worse for wear tonight, man. I know how you feel."

The comment sets my teeth on edge. This guy—I think his name is Evan—perches on the other side of the bar in his fancy suit and presumes to know me? He knows fuck all about *how I feel*. He's just one of the countless patrons who shuffles into a musky bar, hoping their local mixologist will talk them off an emotional ledge. I might be a lot of things, but I'm neither a therapist nor a friend.

I blink and relax my jaw. Christ, I need to chill out. With a deep breath, I wipe down the workspace behind the bar and attempt to be civil. "Just tired."

Evan's a nice guy, perhaps a little too chatty, but he tips like a high-roller. I'm certain he bats for the home team, yet in the few months he's been coming here, he's never hit on me.

"Want another?" I lift my chin in the direction of his empty glass.

He pulls up something on his phone and considers his answer with a furrowed brow.

For a Saturday night, the bar is quieter than it should be. I've worked here since it opened six months ago. Long enough to know that fifty-percent occupancy isn't going to pay the premium rent. I'm beginning to wonder if Blue Dixie has what it takes to survive Manhattan's booming bar scene. More and more buildings are being converted into craft breweries and artsy hipster bars, while Blue Dixie clings to a charming antebellum ambiance that belongs in the South.

This place can burn to the ground for all I care. Except I need this job. I have too many friends struggling to find work, bussing tables, collecting trash, something, *anything* in this pathetic job market. I can't stomach the thought of being unemployed. *Again.*

"I'll have one more." Evan slides the empty glass toward me and rests his forearms on the wooden ledge. "Beats going home to a lonely apartment, you know?"

I do know, but if that was an invitation to go home with him, he's eying the wrong guy.

His dark stubble is thicker than usual, the creases around his eyes deeper. Given his exorbitant tips and high-dollar suits, he's rolling in money. Maybe he spends it all on liquor and drugs, because at the end of the day, the size of the bank account doesn't matter. Life shits on everyone.

An old bearded man two stools down stares into his full pint, seemingly lost in his own woes.

I turn to refill Evan's top-shelf whiskey and collide with Shelby's bony body. She reaches up to touch my chest, and I jerk back with a growl. The owner of Blue Dixie struggles with simple concepts like business ethics and personal space.

"What do you need, Shelby?" I pour Evan's single malt with a scowl in my voice.

"Need to see you in my office." She crowds closer, brushing her hips against mine.

Frizzy bleached hair, wrinkles bracketing her mouth, and underweight in all the wrong areas, she's not my type. In her late thirties, she's ten years my senior. She's also an easy lay—another major point against her.

"I have customers." I pivot away, slide Evan his drink, and move down the bar toward the pretty brunette who just settled in. "What can I get you, gorgeous?"

"Um…" Her gaze travels down my chest, lashes fluttering and cheeks deliciously flushed. "How about something…" Biting down on a nervous smile, she returns to my face. "Hard?"

My dick twitches. Oh, I'll give her hard. If she hangs around till the end of my shift, I'll chase her sweet ass right into her bed and fuck the shyness out of her.

"Decker." Shelby's voice scrapes against my senses. "My office. Now." She waves at the waitress working the tables on the far side of the dark room. "Tracy, can you cover Decker for a few minutes?"

"In five," Tracy calls back and returns to her table.

"Five minutes." Shelby drags an acrylic fingernail down my back. "Don't make me wait."

She sashays toward the rear of the building in a spectacle of black leather, bird legs, and knobby hips.

God only knows what petty bullshit she's contrived this time to get me alone. Every stubborn bone in my body vibrates to leave her waiting all night. But my rent is two months late. If I lose this job, I'm as good as homeless.

I prepare one of my custom cocktails for the pretty brunette, going easy on the Cuban rum and Everclear. I want her sober when she's riding my cock tonight.

"If you're looking for something harder…" I set the wine goblet in front of her. "I'm off the clock at midnight."

I leave her with a startled squeak in her throat and move to the other end of the bar to check on Evan and the quiet bearded guy. Both are nursing their drinks.

"Mind if I ask you a question?" Evan props a fist beneath his chin, studying me with sharp eyes.

"You just did." I focus on filling the drink orders Tracy sent through the system.

"How about a personal question?"

"First Amendment protects your freedom to ask, as well as my freedom to tell you to fuck off."

A smile cracks his face, his dark eyes glittering with interest. "Fuck, if I weren't already committed—"

"I'd still be a straight guy." I move the cocktails to a tray and slide it across the bar to Tracy.

"Thanks." She blows me a kiss. "I'll be back in a couple minutes to cover for you." She tosses her black hair and saunters off, swaying her curvy hips.

I tapped that ass a few times, but I lost interest when the chase turned into *her* chasing *me*.

"Why are you working here?" Evan sips his whiskey.

"Why are you drinking here?"

"You won't like my answer." A vulnerable smile.

I concentrate on mixing drinks, keeping the aggravation out of my tone. "Didn't you just say you were committed?"

I'd rather have a root canal than continue this conversation, but he needs to make his play so I can reject him and move on.

"Committed… Technically, yes." He rubs his

whiskered jaw. "I come here for the view."

His gaze sweeps over me so quickly I almost miss it. Almost.

"Right." I grip the edge of the counter and lean toward him. "Let me make this clear—"

"You have the wrong idea, man. Just hear me out." He reclines against the back of the stool and drums his fingers on the armrest. "You could make so much more money than measly tips in a bar."

I let out a humorless laugh. I already did the whole chase-my-dreams thing. Sank every penny and second of my life into it. Ten years of blood and sweat left me bankrupt, betrayed, and sick to my soul.

"I'm serious. Look at them." Evan tilts his chin at the tables of women across the room. "They can't keep their eyes off you. And the meek little mouse at the end of the bar? I'm pretty sure she soaked her panties the instant you looked at her. Not to mention the lady boner your boss is sporting beneath her skirt. Every woman in this place is breathlessly aware of you."

I don't like where he's going with this. "If you're suggesting that I whore myself…" My blood heats. "I'm fucking offended."

Two stools down, the old man lifts his head, narrows beady eyes, and returns to his full pint.

"You're an idiot if you don't know how ridiculously good-looking you are." Evan openly and leisurely peruses me from head to groin. "You could model."

"Vanity's a neurotic disorder." I already have enough personality problems.

Why does he care anyway? I'm not used to this weird role reversal. Usually, the guy bellying up to the bar is asking me for advice, not giving it.

I move to the computer screen and print out his check. It's time for Evan to go.

"How about stripping?" He smirks.

If he knew what I used to do for a living, he'd swallow his fucking tongue.

I slap the bill on the counter in front of him. "Have a good night."

Moving to the other end of the bar, I focus on the brunette. "How's the drink?"

With a timid smile, she nods stiffly, wrestling to maintain eye contact. Women like her, all delicate bones and bashful glances, tend to be hellcats in bed. My dick pulses at the thought of defiling her long and laboriously.

"Hurry back, Decker." Tracy slides in behind me and covertly caresses my ass. "I have tables waiting."

I knock her hand away. That's the problem with boning women I have to see again. Once I let them touch, they never stop.

On my way to the back room, I wink at a table of gawking women. They blush and sigh, and their giggling whispers follow me down the hall. Maybe I *should* strip. Can't seem to stop myself from flirting with uncharted territory. I love the hunt, but once I catch them and fuck them, I'm done. I blame it on the male sex drive and the primal need to spread my seed.

When I reach the office, I lean against the door frame and rest my fingers in the back pockets of my jeans. "What's up?"

"Close the door." Shelby glides around the desk, her expression a bit too eager for comfort.

"Close it yourself." I give her a bored look.

"While your orneriness is unacceptable out on the floor..." She sidles up to me and reaches back to shut the door. "I'd love to rile up your temper between the sheets."

I cringe at her proximity. She smells like all my drunken regrets. Good thing I've never been drunk enough to add her to that list.

"Not interested." I brace an arm against the door above her head, preventing her from closing it. "What do you need?"

Her bottom lip pouts out. "Don't play hard to get, Decker."

I don't have the energy for this. As I turn to walk out, she cups me between the legs and purrs.

My muscles tense, and before I can stop myself, I grab her neck and slam her against the office wall.

"Touch me again," I seethe past clenched teeth, "and I'll file a sexual harassment charge."

"Do it." She claws at my hand around her throat, her eyes glistening with fear. "The camera in the ceiling will back up my assault charge against you."

Goddammit. I release her and glare at the lens in the upper corner of the room. "What the fuck do you want?"

She rubs the fingerprint marks on her neck. "You fuck every woman I hire." Her shoulders curl forward, and she shoves them back. "I've been more than patient. It's my turn."

Jesus fucking Christ, she's clueless. But I spare her the hurtful words and give her the full force of my glare.

She stands taller. "I'll make it good for you."

I shake my head, repulsed. "You're standing at the starting line, holding on to an abstract notion. Call it gratification, victory, whatever—that's the finish line. What you don't see is the race, the intensity in the pursuit, the competition. And the male ego's huge fucking hard-on when he wins the prize."

Her face contorts. "I see everything, dammit. I've spent six months watching you chase every woman but me!"

She's been throwing herself at me since the day she hired me. She doesn't get it, and at this point, she never will. Cruelty is the only way she'll leave me the fuck alone.

"Give me a raise." I flick my gaze up and down her anorexic body. "Put on some weight, lose ten years, show some fucking dignity, and I *might* consider a hand job."

Her breath catches, and she stabs a blood-red fingernail at the open door. "Get out!"

"Gladly." I stride toward the hall.

"Don't come back." Tears thicken her voice. "You're fired, asshole."

I stop just outside the office, ears ringing and insides exploding.

Fired?

She fucking fired me. Now would be a good time to seduce her. I could do it with a flick of my tongue. One kiss and she'd melt against me. Followed by her mouth around my cock, my job reinstated with a pay raise, and probably the night off. In her bed.

I shudder. That would be a new low, even for me.

My breath quickens. Rent's overdue. Electricity's already shut off. Forget the astronomical attorney fees I'll never catch up on. What about food? Do I have enough tip money to eat for a couple days?

I'm so fucked.

Fury and dread coalesces into a vicious tyrant beneath my skin. My arm swings out, and my fist collides with the hollow door, splintering the wood, shooting pain up my arm, and leaving a satisfying hole.

"That'll come out of your wages," she shrieks.

"Fuck you." I storm down the hall, hands shaking and pulse hammering.

Grabbing my leather jacket from the break room, I slow my gait through the maze of high-top tables and target the brunette at the bar. A younger man sits beside her with an arm around the back of her seat. Perfect distraction for my rage. I shrug on my jacket and prowl toward them.

The thing about the chase is I don't care if it's quick or slow, as long as there's an effort. A conquest. A victorious *win*. Fuck participation trophies. I want the gold fucking medal.

I step behind her and swivel the stool to position her toward me and away from the man tickling her hair with his mustache.

Keeping my hands on the armrests, I lean in and touch her with only my voice. "I'm in a mood, gorgeous. The kind of mood that guarantees hours of hard…focused…pleasure." I breathe each word at her ear, low and full of heat. "You can try your luck with the mustache or you can follow me out."

"That man just assaulted me," Shelby screeches across the bar. "Get the hell out, Decker, or I'm calling the cops."

I step back, and the brunette clutches the front of her blouse, lips parted, breaths shallow, and eyes dazed.

I could convince her to follow me with just a few more words, but something inside me pulls back. I can't be gentle tonight, and this woman is sweet and delicate. She deserves better.

Without taking her eyes off me, she blindly reaches for her purse and shifts toward the edge of the seat, trembling with uncertainty yet gravitating. *Toward me.* She's a breath away from surrender, and I'm tempted. So fucking tempted.

"Another night, sweetheart." I brush a thumb across her bottom lip and head toward the front door.

In my periphery, Evan throws a wad of bills on the counter and chases after me. A chase I'm not interested in.

I don't slow as I hit the sidewalk and stride toward the subway, my exhales steaming in the chilly air.

"Decker!" His footfalls close in behind me. "Wait up."

"Get lost, Evan." I pick up my pace, eyes forward and hands shoved in the pockets of my jacket.

"I have a proposition." He catches up and darts into my path.

Like I need another *proposition*. I veer around him, and he moves with me, his expression hard with determination. We do a blisterfeld dance on the crowded crosswalk, shuffling side to side in my attempt to pass him.

Exasperated, I shove him away and charge toward the subway tunnel a block ahead.

A dark unheated apartment waits for me in Greenwich Village. No electricity or food, but I still have a bed. Might as well enjoy it, since I'll have to evacuate the place as soon as tomorrow.

My stomach tumbles. What the hell am I going to do? Without family or friends to take me in, I'm back where I started a year ago.

Rock.

Fucking.

Bottom.

With time, I'll find another shit job, but not before I'm evicted and back on the street without a pot to piss in. Thanks to a string of misfortune and a few poor life choices, I'm the quintessence of an Eminem song. Maybe my worthless mother was right. She'd love to see me move all my belongings into the pit of *never-gonna-amount-to-anything* and make a home there.

"Decker," Evan calls after me. "I can get you an interview."

That halts my feet.

"An interview for what?" I turn and find him standing several feet away, hands anchored on his hips.

"Have you eaten tonight?" He points at the narrow cross street that cuts through to Ninth Avenue. "There's an Italian place. A little dive in a basement. Kind of rough around the edges, but they make the best gnocchi."

"I know the place." My mouth waters, but I can't afford a meal there. "What's the job?"

"I'll tell you over dinner." He cocks his head. "My treat."

The offer smells sketchy and underhanded, and I always trust my nose. "See you around, Evan."

I pivot toward the subway tunnel, my throat tightening with each step.

"They'll pay you for the interview," Evan says, still standing where I left him. "All you have to do is apply and show up."

I stop at the stairway that leads down to the subway and grip the railing. What kind of employer pays applicants for an interview?

Evan doesn't know me from Adam. Doesn't

know my prior work experience or qualifications. Hell, he just heard Shelby announce to the whole fucking bar that I assaulted her.

Warning bells sound in my head, spurring my feet down the stairs.

"Five thousand dollars." His footsteps sound behind me, followed by a hand on my arm.

I don't shrug him off, because fuck me, five thousand dollars would cover my overdue rent. It would mean the difference between a bed and park bench.

"What do I have to do?" Suspicion growls through my voice.

Expression softening, he nods in the direction of the Italian restaurant. "Dinner."

Chapter 2

Decker

I stretch my legs beneath the table, staring at the screen on Evan's phone. The website he pulled up lists the senior leaders at the New York Presbyterian Hospital. Evan's clean-shaved face smiles among the photos of suit-and-tie executives. I'm reluctantly impressed, despite the confusion pounding my head.

Evan Daniels, MD

Chief Operating Officer

Beneath his title is a bio of his prestigious education and work experience. Evidently, he was a cardiologist before he joined the board of directors at New York's top rated hospital.

The url looks legit. Why is he showing this to me?

"You can get me an interview at the hospital?" I slide his phone across the table. "What's the job?"

Janitorial? Security guard? Does it matter? The possibility of employment curls a tendril of hope through me, but the rational voice in the back of my mind swats it away. They won't hire me when they research my background. Besides, janitors aren't paid five grand for an interview.

"The interview isn't at the hospital." He rests a hand on the rim of his water glass, poking a finger at the floating ice cubes. "I showed you the web page to make a point. I have a legitimate job, one that's public and *sensitive*. I have a reputation to protect."

Fuck, that sounds ominous. I recline in the chair and slug back a gulp of beer. "Go on."

His gaze darts around the room. The dozen other tables sit empty. We're the only diners in the tiny restaurant.

Our balding waiter bends over the pastry counter near the exit, snapping in hushed tones at the silver-haired woman who seated us. She huffs and rolls her eyes, speaking in heated Italian. He throws his arms in the air and vanishes into the kitchen through a side door.

"The owners." Evan grins, removing his gaze from the woman and placing it on me. "Married forty-five years. Always bickering and hopelessly in love." His expression sobers. "What I'm about to tell you can't be repeated."

I laugh, a shocked sound that I quickly cut off. "I don't know what this is, but—"

"Shut up and listen." He rakes a hand through his thinning black hair. "I told you I was committed." His eyes find mine. "But I haven't met my companion yet."

Wow. Okay. Something's wrong with this guy. Is he not right in the head? If he hadn't shown me his work credentials, I would've walked out. Instead, I squint at him, silently prompting him to continue.

"I just came out of a relationship. An *agreement*. My partner...he...uh, reunited with his ex and didn't renew our agreement." Pain clouds his eyes, and he blinks. "So I signed a second agreement, got matched with a new companion. I'll meet him when he moves into my place next week."

"What?" I lean forward, voice low. "You contract your relationships?" I shake my head, baffled. "Why?"

"It's…more efficient. I work long hours and—"

The waiter shuffles out of the kitchen, carrying a tray of food piping with steam. The aroma of garlic and pesto permeates the air as he serves two dishes of gnocchi, tops off our waters, and replaces my beer with a new one. He returns to the kitchen with his wife on his heels, leaving Evan and me alone in tense silence.

"Eat." Evan picks up a fork, stabs a dumpling, and scoots it through the white sauce. "I'm a client of an exclusive company that provides companionship to a small network of people like me. People who can afford to invest in arranged relationships."

Exclusive service. Arranged relationships. Five grand for an interview. The proposal he hasn't spelled out hits me sideways. He's talking about male escorts. It can't be anything else. I choke on a bite of pasta and press a fist against my chest.

"Already told you." I reach for the glass of water and drain it in an attempt to cool my rising temper. "I'm not whoring—"

"It's not a brothel." His eyes harden. "They don't sell sex by the hour—"

"But they *do* sell sex." I jerk forward, bracing an elbow on the table. "You brought me here to propose I become a gigolo for some secret society of doctors and rich folks? I don't have a problem with your sexual orientation, could care less where you put your dick. But I will *not* let a man fuck me, not even for money."

I might've reached rock bottom, but I won't go there. Not ever.

"It's not like that." His face reddens. "There are female clients. Infidelity is a respectable—"

"Infidelity?" My smirk feels more like a grimace. "Appropriate."

"Are you going to let me talk?"

I shrug. "It's your wasted breath." I dig into the gnocchi, my hope for employment crushed like everything else in my life.

"Look, I've tried the dating sites, the bar hookups, the friend-of-a-friend connections." He takes a bite, chews slowly, and swallows with a scowl. "I can't seem to hang on to someone longer than a few weeks." A self-deprecating smile. "Funny how I can treat every heart condition known to man, but when it comes to relationships, I always end up with a guy hellbent on destroying my heart." He rubs his forehead and sighs. "That's why Infidelity is so appealing. They have a remarkable ability to pair clients like me with an employee who fits."

"If that's the case, why are you on your second contract?"

"*Agreement.* That's what they call it. And my situation is uncommon. My companion…" He closes his eyes for a brief moment. "We were perfect together. He would've stayed and renewed the agreement, but…"

"The ex."

"Yeah." He stabs his fork a little too forcibly in a dumpling. "He shared five years with the ex. Only a year with me. So when the ex showed back up—"

"Wait. Did you say a *year*?" My eyes widen. "The agreement can last that long?"

"One year is mandatory." The corner of his mouth lifts. "Relationships aren't built in a pay-by-the-hour motel room."

"I want a job, not a fucking relationship." I glower at my plate of pasta, appetite gone. "Thanks for dinner." *Where's the waiter?* "I'm gonna get this boxed up and head—"

"Take the interview. *Then* make your decision. If you don't like what they tell you, you'll walk away with five Gs, no strings attached."

A knot of too-good-to-be-true coils in my stomach. "You know those timeshare scams? The kind where they offer you spectacular prizes for sitting through a one-hour presentation, which turns into an all-day sales pitch that leaves you brainwashed and broke?" I finish off my beer. "Your one hour is up."

"No offense, but I get the feeling you're already broke." His gaze roams my face with too much scrutiny. "And you don't strike me as someone who's easily manipulated."

True, but desperate men do desperate things. I reach for my beer and remember it's empty. "What do you get out of this?"

"Nothing—which is everything. I was in a bad headspace a year ago. After a string of rough breakups, I beat myself up, was convinced something was wrong with me. Then a friend stepped in, an acquaintance in my social circle. He gave me a similar pitch to the one I'm giving you. It changed my life. I can't pay him back, but I can pay it forward." His gaze fastens on mine, steady and incisive. "Infidelity operates on word-of-mouth only. Confidentiality is vital, and employees must be sponsored. I want to be that person for you. Your sponsor. Because despite how my last agreement ended, the past year with Chr…uh, with my companion was the best year of my life."

"A secret network that's invite-only." I laugh. What I should be doing is walking out that door, but curiosity keeps my ass in the chair. "Sounds like Fight Club rules."

"Exactly. Most of the clients are distinguished

and well-known. We're talking CEOs, politicians, celebrities—people who spend a lot of money shielding their private affairs from the public eye. If you're ever asked about Infidelity, you say you don't know. You do *not* acknowledge it outside of the network."

"You don't know me." I lower my voice and lean closer, glaring at him. "I can sell your dirty sex life to the newspaper and destroy your career."

"I've been watching you sling beer at Blue Dixie for six months." He smiles softly. "My fascination might've started as a crush, but I swear I'm not a creepy stalker or anything like that." He strokes a thumb along the rim of his plate. "You have a way with people. Everything about you is magnetic and attractive—your confidence, your charm, your irresistible sex appeal. With assets like that at your disposal, you could woo a wealthy woman out of every penny she has." His lips twist then flatten in a line. "But you'd never do that. Beneath that fuck-off exterior lies a tremendous amount of honor and self-respect."

My skin tingles uncomfortably. "You don't know that."

"Remember when I slipped in a hundred-dollar bill with my check?"

Yeah, I thought it was a mistake and caught him on his way out the door to give it back. "No one tips like that at Blue Dixie."

"You could've kept it, played it off like it was a tip and not a slip-up on my part."

"You were testing me?"

He nods. "You never hit on a married woman, not even when her interest in you is blindingly obvious." Something akin to respect shines in his eyes. "I wouldn't be sitting here with you if I wasn't one-hundred-percent confident in your integrity." He sighs. "Maybe I'm being presumptuous, but you can have anyone you want. Yet you seem so…"

I arch a brow.

"Lonely." He looks down at his plate, twisting the fork. "I know you need a job, but part of me hopes you'll consider this interview and find happiness in the company of another person."

Loneliness is so far down on my list of problems right now. I'm unemployed and soon-to-be evicted with twelve bucks in my bank account. I *need* that five thousand dollars.

I rub the back of my neck. "Some of the clients are female?"

"Of course." His eyes light up, and he sits taller. "You can restrict your profile to women."

"Attractive, young, physically fit women?" A hot corporate type who needs a stiff dick at the end of a long work day? I can get behind something like that.

"You don't get to pick your client. Infidelity prides itself in its mastery of pairing people based on personalities and tastes. They're so good at it, in fact, they only offer their clients two agreements. Two chances to make it work."

"You're on your second agreement. What if that doesn't pan out?"

"I'm out. While clients are allowed two agreements, employees only get one. Infidelity doesn't pimp. This isn't an escort service. Clients aren't paying for companions who are rotated in and out. They're paired with an employee who's never done this before. It's genius if you think about it."

"How much do *you* pay for this exclusivity?" I can't imagine paying for sex.

"That's not something I can talk about. I can promise you an interview, but Infidelity decides whether to hire you. They have a very selective intake process, which includes medical tests, psych evaluations, and background investigations. The last thing their clients need is a scandal involving an Infidelity employee with a shady past." He tilts his head. "Full disclosure is advised. If you're hiding something, they'll find it."

His unasked question hangs in the air, but I'm not about to air my dirty laundry to a stranger.

"If they offer you a job," he says, "you'll receive a monthly check from them. Most clients provide housing, meals, all the basic expenses on top of your Infidelity salary. For example, if you're required to attend black tie affairs, the client would cover the wardrobe and attendance fees. You can potentially go the entire year without spending a dime of your income from Infidelity. At the end of the year, the agreement can be renewed. Or it can be bought out, if you and the client decide to stay together without the company. Or it can be terminated. In that case, you receive a severance package and walk away with the money you saved during the year."

"What's the pay?" Am I actually considering this?

"It varies. I'm not sure I'm supposed to—"

"Give me a rough idea. What did they pay your last companion?"

He shifts in the chair, takes a sip from his water, and meets my eyes. "Twenty thousand dollars a month."

CHAPTER 3

Decker

"Sorry?" My heart stops then restarts in a frenzied tempo. "Can you repeat that?"

"If you're hired…" Evan swallows the last bite of his pasta. "You'll earn around twenty grand a month."

I don't even try to hide the frozen shock on my face. My entire body ignites in a state of excited desperation. I force my brain to focus on the downside, because no one offers that kind of salary without a huge fucking trade-off.

"You said Infidelity decides the pairings." I slide my uneaten dinner aside and rest my forearms on the table. "I could end up with…" I grasp for a realistic albeit exaggerated scenario. "A fat old lady with a fetish for strap-ons and gimp masks."

"Maybe?" His lips twitch. "When you fill out your profile, you can set certain restrictions, such as no bondage, no anal, stuff like that. As the company's name suggests, some clients are married, but you can request a single woman. Just don't expect to be matched with your ideal body type. Remember you're the employee, providing a service to Infidelity's client. And unless the client decides to share you with another, monogamy is mandatory."

"Christ." I swipe a hand down my face, grimacing as I picture a four-hundred-pound grandma in black leather. "Call me shallow, but I have standards."

"Are those standards worth adjusting for twenty thousand a month?"

Maybe, but there's no way I'll get it up for a woman who turns my stomach. "What if I sign the agreement, meet the client, and can't go through with it?"

"You're stuck with her for a year, man. The only time agreements end early is when there's abuse. Non-consensual bodily harm isn't tolerated."

Given what I used to do for a living, I have zero concern about someone wailing on me. But one year? Fuck, that's a long time to share a bed with a fugly woman. Because realistically, how many wealthy, sexy, young women pay for sex? Why would they? Men probably make up most of Infidelity's clientele, and those few women who pay for companionship are undoubtedly lacking in physical looks or personality. Probably both.

The waiter emerges from the kitchen, and I grab my empty beer bottle and hold it up for him.

"You want anything?" I ask Evan.

"I'll stick with water. Gotta work in the morning."

Wish I could say the same.

We sit through a thoughtful span of silence until the waiter brings another beer and the check and returns to the kitchen.

"No matter what you decide…" Evan loosens the knot on his tie and leans back, slinging a leg over the other. "Be judicious about the privacy of this company and its associates. If you ever encounter another Infidelity client or employee, you can't mention my name. Not to anyone except the intake representative."

"You don't need to worry about that." I sip the beer. "I have no intention or reason to sabotage you."

"Thanks." He fidgets with the end of his tie. "Where's your head at on all of this?"

"All over the damn place." But my appetite's returned, so I pull the plate back in front of me and finish off the lukewarm gnocchi.

"Don't overthink it, Decker. You need a job. The client is paying for companionship, but she goes into this fully aware your incentive is money. And who knows? You might come out of this with a hard-on for lumpy, blue-haired ladies wearing strap-ons."

He chuckles, and I laugh at the absurdity of it, instantly feeling less tense. The more I consider the interview, the lighter I feel. Infidelity's a solution. If I'm honest, it's the best option I've had in a long time. My hang-up is the sex. I've never done monogamy. Never fucked a woman I wasn't attracted to. Granted, some of those women turned into regrets, but that's on me. I was the one in control. I *need* that power, the ability to say when, who, and how.

Though I guess there are worse things than spending a year satisfying an unpleasant woman. Like giving ten-dollar blowjobs in dark alleys. Thankfully, I've never hit that kind of low, but if I find myself homeless and starving, fuck knows what I'd do for a meal. I have too many desperate friends doing unspeakable things to make ends meet.

"Tell me about the interview." I set the fork down, my plate scraped clean. "Do I have to perform?"

"Perform…? You mean sex?"

I nod. "How else are they going to assess my qualifications?"

"God, no. Not like that." His face pinches. "After a background check and medical exams, all that's left is a conversation with the intake representative."

Sounds painless, but I've only been unemployed for an hour. I should exhaust other options first, like finding another bartender gig. Except I've been actively looking for a better job for the past year. Opportunities are pathetic.

"I need to think about it," I say.

"Yes, of course." He grabs his phone. "I just need a way to contact you. What's your number?"

I dig through the pocket of my jacket where it hangs on my chair and remove my phone. The screen doesn't respond, the battery dead. My electricity's shut off, so charging it is a problem. Then I remember the prepaid plan ran out this morning. I intended to refill it tomorrow, but that won't be happening.

With a heavy exhale, I drop the useless thing on the table. "Give me your number, and I'll contact you if I'm interested."

His lips form a flat line. He's probably considering the fact that once I walk out the door, he'll have no way to reach me and might never see me again.

"No job means…" I return the phone to the pocket of my jacket. "No more cell service."

"How are you going to call me if you don't have a phone?"

I lift a shoulder. "I can use a neighbor's phone." Except I might not have neighbors after tomorrow.

"Say *yes* to the interview, Decker." His fingers clench and relax on his phone. "I can call the Infidelity rep right now, schedule the medical appointments and interview. No further contact is needed."

"Don't I need to fill out an application?" One that

will ask about my prior work experience and criminal history. My pulse kicks up.

"You can do it on my phone after I make the call."

"I don't know." What kind of man am I to even consider this? I feel like I'm losing control of my life, and I fucking hate it. "I need to think—"

"Five thousand dollars for a couple hours of your time." His jaw sets, eyes tight with impatience. "What exactly do you need to think about?"

He's right. My scandalous past might prevent me from being hired, but if what he's saying is true, I'll receive enough money to get by until I find a real job.

"They'll pay me for the interview, even if they don't hire me?" I ask.

"Yes."

"Fine." I blow out a breath. "Make the goddamn call."

A victorious smile spreads across his face, but there's no smugness there. This guy is genuinely happy. *For me*. It's mind-boggling.

He stands and paces away from the table with the phone at his ear. I drain my beer while he sets up the appointments, ends the call, and returns to the table.

"Well?" I fold my arms across my chest.

He removes a business card and a pen from the pocket inside his suit jacket and jots down times and addresses on the back.

"Medical and psychological exams tomorrow morning." He hands me the card. "Interview the day after. If something comes up, my office number is on the other side. Let's get that application going."

Twenty minutes later, I click *submit* on the electronic form and return the phone to him.

"You'll be at the interview?" I stand and pull on my leather jacket.

"I'll be there as your sponsor." Having already paid the bill, he walks with me to the door. "Wear a tie."

I own exactly one suit, worn to dozens of interviews over the past year. I despise the damn thing, but I'll get over it.

Outside, we pause on the sidewalk, hands stuffed in our coat pockets and breaths mingling in white clouds between us.

"It's fucking cold." I tense against the shivery night air.

"Do you have heat at your—?"

"I'll manage." I back away, in the direction of the subway. "Hey, thanks for dinner."

"Yeah. Anytime..." He stares at his feet, jaw wriggling as if working up the nerve to ask me something.

I can guess it involves me going back to his place.

"See you in a couple days." I turn and tread down the dim street, saving him from an awkward rejection.

That night, I stretch beneath the blankets on my small mattress, flipping the business card between my fingers. The frigid darkness of my five-hundred-square-foot studio apartment aggravates my fraying nerves. At least I still have warm water for tomorrow's shower.

The medical tests in the morning will be a waste of time. I don't touch drugs, have never had sex without a condom, and don't suffer from mental illness. It's the background investigation that'll put the brakes on a twenty-grand-per-month job offer. If Infidelity's clients are as high-profile as Evan claims, they won't go near me and the shit storm I was caught up in. My name was cleared of all involvement, but my reputation is fucked so badly I'll never work in the industry again.

At least I don't have to contemplate having sex with an undesirable woman. I'll go to the interview, collect the five grand, and forget about Infidelity.

As I set Evan's business card on the floor beside the mattress, a worrisome thought hits me. He never asked for my last name. Wouldn't he need it to set up the interview? I included it on my application, but that was after he set the appointments.

I stab a hand through my hair. If he already knew my name, he knows the rest. All it takes is a Google search on Decker Gabrielli to fall into a wasteland of negative press. Yet he set up the interview anyway? Without asking for the details surrounding my fall to shame?

My breaths quicken. Does that mean he's not concerned about it? That Infidelity might actually consider me? Christ, if they offered me a job, would I even accept?

Twenty grand a month.

Free rent and food for a year.

Three-hundred-and-sixty-five days of sex with a repulsive woman.

I don't know whether to laugh or freak the fuck out.

CHAPTER 4

Decker

Two days later, I stand outside a curved building that matches the address Evan gave me. Scrutinizing my reflection in the blue-glass door, I straighten my tie and brush out the suit jacket. The buttoned collar strangles my neck, my skin itchy and overheated despite the wintry blasts of wind. I'm so fucking ready to be done with this charade.

While yesterday's visit to the medical office was painless, I spent last night mulling over the damn interview. The nurse called me Mr. Gabrielli. If she had access to my full name, Evan did, too. No doubt he investigated my past. Maybe he's optimistic about Infidelity hiring me despite my slandered reputation, but I remain more conflicted than ever about whether I'd accept a sketchy job offer.

The landlord gave me until tonight to pay her the overdue rent or turn in my key. I'll have a few dollars left after I hand over the interview money. That's if Infidelity cuts me a check before I leave today. I have no fucking clue what I'll do tomorrow or the day after. I haven't been able to focus past this interview.

I step inside the large lobby and spot Evan in the sitting area. His smile's as bright as his eyes.

"You know about Adam Lamont," I say in greeting.

His grin falters but doesn't fade. "Yes." He leads me to the wall of elevators.

"Then you know my association with him." I keep my voice low, eyes on an older man who waits for an elevator a few feet away. "You know what Adam did?"

"Yes." Evan slides a hand down his tie. "I also know he's in prison, and you're not. Did the judge make a mistake?"

"Fuck no." I grind my teeth and whisper harshly, "But I was his partner. That shit was happening right under my nose, and I didn't stop it."

"Because you didn't know, right?" Evan gives me a hard look.

A familiar fist of shame clenches inside me. *I should've known, should've paid better attention.*

The elevator closest to the older man opens. We follow him in, and Evan pushes the button for the 37th floor. Since we're not alone, I keep my mouth shut during the ride up.

We arrive at our floor, and Evan leads me to the receptionist behind a glass desk. *Infidelity* scrolls in huge curly letters across the wall behind her. When I filled out the on-line application at the restaurant, Evan explained that the privately-run Fortune 500 company is a website that offers a number of services to exclusive clients.

But the service I'm interviewing for isn't one they promote on the web.

I lean a hip against the desk as Evan speaks with the receptionist. She takes down his name and makes a call, her gaze flitting repeatedly to me, her cheeks flushed and lashes lowered coyly.

"You don't even have to try," Evan whispers

while she's on the phone.

I shrug. If the girl knows why I'm here, she's probably imagining me fucking random clients who have stopped by her desk.

A moment later, a middle-aged woman rounds the corner and extends a hand to Evan. "Good morning, Mr. Daniels. So good to see you."

"Ms. Flores. Thanks for fitting us in." He shakes her hand and turns to me. "This is Decker Gabrielli. Decker, meet Karen Flores."

She stands taller, her shrewd gaze sweeping me from head to toe. Not in a pervy way. More like she's taking my measure. When she returns to my face, her smile is warm, her expression open, perhaps even enthusiastic.

She's not bad looking for an older lady. Her stiff skirt suit is a bit off-putting, but there are some wicked curves beneath the polyester.

"Mr. Gabrielli." She grasps my offered hand. "It's a pleasure."

"The pleasure's mine."

Instead of flinching at the pressure of my grip, she returns the squeeze with impressive strength.

"If you'll follow me…" She leads us down a hall, through a labyrinth of private offices and cubicles, and swipes a badge over the sensor beside another elevator. "How are you doing, Evan?" Her voice is soft, asking more than her words imply.

"I've been better." He tucks his hands in his pockets. "I miss him."

I don't really know Evan, but my gut tells me his kindness is genuine. I hope Infidelity doesn't give him false hope in his second agreement. He deserves happiness.

"We couldn't have predicted…" She straightens her suit jacket. "When we hired him, his ex was out of the picture."

"I know." He smiles sadly. "There's no blame here."

When the doors open, we file in, and she presses the button labeled *I*. The only other option is *O* – the floor we're on.

"*I* and *O*?" I raise an eyebrow. "Is that some kind of secret binary code?"

"Mm," she answers, which isn't an answer at all.

The elevator moves, and the popping sensation in my ears suggests we're speeding toward the top of the building.

"Does it stand for *in* and *out*?" I clasp my hands behind my back. "Could be an interesting innuendo. Do you repeat that in your head every time you're in here? In and out. In and out."

Evan stares at his feet, shaking his head, while Karen bites her lip, her expression otherwise neutral.

"No?" I wink at her. "I bet you think it from now on."

"Charming, Mr. Gabrielli," she says as the elevator stops on *I*. "Right this way."

I step into another swank lobby with another glass desk, receptionist, and an *Infidelity* sign on the wall. Instead of corridors leading off into a maze of offices, there's only one door, secured with a keypad.

Passcodes are only necessary when there's something worth protecting. Like secrets. I bet the *I* and *O* in the elevator represent *inside* and *outside* the true Infidelity, and I'm now standing in the inner core of the company.

Karen enters a code and leads us into a classy

office with a large desk, leather chairs, and rich wood cabinets. A wall of windows frames the glitter and stone of Manhattan's financial district. At another—less desperate—point in my life, I might've appreciated the view, but I'm not here to be impressed and wooed. If Infidelity doesn't pay me for the interview today, my ass is homeless.

I trail after her toward the desk. "About the payment for today—"

"The receptionist will have a check for you on your way out." She lowers into the chair behind the desk.

"Thank you." Tension loosens from my shoulders, making the tie feel a little less tight.

"You're welcome. I suspected there might be some urgency given your situation."

Situation. That's one word for it.

"If you're thirsty, help yourself to the wet bar." Karen opens a laptop and taps the mouse pad. "There's water, coffee, and spirits." She nods at the built-in cabinet on the far wall. "Since you're a bartender, I assume you're particular about how your drinks are made."

It's ten in the morning. Does she think I'm a lush?

Anxious to get this over with, I sit beside Evan in the chair facing her desk. "I'm sure you're aware that as of two days ago, I'm no longer a bartender."

"Yes." She slides the laptop to the side and clasps her hands together on the desk. "Decker Gabrielli. Twenty-eight years old. High school diploma. Average grades. No college. Recently fired from Blue Dixie." She tilts her head. "Not the most impressive résumé. Which makes the success of your business venture remarkable."

My chest clenches. "If you call it a success, you haven't done your homework."

"Oh, I'd say *Contender Sports* did extremely well. Three store fronts in just a few years. Investors lined up at your door. Prime real estate. You had a gym right here in Manhattan, did you not?"

"Yeah." Resentment bubbles up, gnawing just as sharply as it had a year ago when I lost everything.

"It was an ingenious idea," she says. "While many would love to learn MMA fighting—"

"Combat sports, not cage fighting." I glance at Evan's unreadable expression and return to Karen. "We taught boxing, Muay Thai, and wrestling to serious students. Some were on track for the Olympics."

"My mistake." She narrows her eyes. "My point is that most people aren't willing to spend money on themselves, not to learn a new skill like boxing. But the sky's the limit when it comes to investing in sports activities for their children. That's one of the reasons your business did so well."

It's also why it failed. I hold her stare, despite the shame tightening my throat.

"Your business partner, Adam Lamont," she says, focusing on the laptop screen, "was sentenced to seventy-five years in prison for three counts of sexual abuse and sodomy with children under the age of ten. You were exonerated of all involvement."

"Tell that to the parents who pulled their kids out of my schools." Within months of the initial charges, I went from three-thousand students to zero. Resentment surges through my veins and roughens my voice. "Doesn't matter that the charges weren't against me. I ran a sports school geared toward children with a pedophilic instructor. *That* is on me."

"I understand how that would negatively impact your ability to bring in new business." She gentles her voice. "It also explains why you have no personal references on your application."

I smirk to stifle what would've been a disgusted expression. Since discovering that my best friend is a child molester, I've deliberately kept everyone at a distance. "I'm not as trusting as I used to be."

"Understandable. But from a legal standpoint, you're innocent. Ergo, Infidelity doesn't consider you a risk in a high-profile relationship."

"What are you saying?" I straighten in the chair, my mind spinning. "Are you actually considering me?"

"Mr. Gabrielli—"

"Decker."

"Decker, tell me why Infidelity should hire you."

I'm not prepared for this and grapple for how to respond. "You want the bullshit answer or the honest one?"

"Honesty is the *only* answer."

When I meet Evan's burning eyes, I'm certain he's silently begging me to filter my words. But I don't want this job, for so many reasons.

"You shouldn't hire me." I recline in the chair and prop a foot on a knee. "I'm here for the five grand. Nothing more."

"I see." She purses her lips. "Will you go back to bartending?"

"I'll find something."

"And when your next boss sexually harasses you? What happens then?"

My foot drops to the floor, and I glare at Evan.

"I didn't…" His eyes widen, head shaking. "I didn't know the details."

"I saw the video feed at Blue Dixie." She drums her fingers lightly on the keyboard.

"How the hell did you get that?" My pulse speeds up. Who are these people?

"We're resourceful." She tucks a strand of hair behind her ear. "I saw how and *where* the owner put her hands on you, so I'll overlook the aggressive way you handled it. That said, Infidelity has zero tolerance for abuse. If you touch a client out of anger or in any way that could be construed as assault, you're finished."

"You don't need to worry about that. I'm not interested in your—"

"What is it about Infidelity that has your mind made up?"

"I have enough shame in my past, don't you think? Do you know how difficult it is to get a job when your name is smeared? Everyone knows how to Google, even bar owners. They do a quick search, find my name associated with a convicted child molester, and toss my application in the trash. Why bother researching the truth when there's a hundred other applications on their desk?" My hands fist and relax. "I don't need to add *sexual services*—or whatever it is you employ here—to my already vile résumé."

I expect her to close the laptop and send me packing. Instead she steeples her fingers against her mouth and studies me for a silent moment.

Eventually, she bends forward, elbows on the desk. "I assume Evan gave you an overview of exactly what we do here, but I'll make it crystal clear. We do *not* sell sexual services. Our clients are the elite of the elite, and they pay for a companion who represents their sophistication, a partner who won't embarrass them in public, and a relationship that's mutually enjoyed in private. That's why compatibility and pairing the right personalities is crucial, and we're very good at it."

Mutually enjoyed? For an entire year? Not likely. "You're telling me you'd put me with someone I can tolerate?"

"I'm *guaranteeing* you'll be paired with someone you enjoy."

"How? The application didn't ask for my preferences. You have no idea who and what I enjoy."

The form focused on limits, triggers, sexual orientation and practices, and relationship history. My answers could be summed up to *straight man with an aversion to anal and monogamy.* That tells her nothing.

"Let's see..." She looks directly in my eyes. "I know you can sweet talk your way into any woman's bed, but you prefer a challenge—"

"Why would you—?"

"The chase is your favorite part. Once you catch them, you lose interest."

"None of that was on the application." I stand and pace to the windows behind her desk, my nerves raw with suspicion. "Are you stalking me?"

"We have over a hundred employees, all of them selected through careful screening." She swivels her chair, facing me. "I excel at my job, Decker, because if I disappoint a client, or worse, if I create a scandal in his or her life, they have the power to destroy everything we've built here. Our clients are influential, extremely wealthy, and they pay a premium for the highest level of service and confidentiality. Their friends and family don't even know about us. Which is why I make it my business to know my employees."

I cross my arms and lean a shoulder against the floor-to-ceiling glass. "Why would Infidelity want to hire a guy like me?"

"You're physically appealing. If I may be so bold, you're the epitome of masculine virility. There isn't a client in our portfolio who wouldn't be taken with you."

Her smarmy sales pitch makes my insides curl, and I consciously force myself to relax.

"You caught Evan's eye," she says, "and he's picky."

Evan fidgets with the cuff of his sleeve. "I'm not..."

She arches a brow.

"Okay, yeah, I'm picky." He blows out a breath. "I also have a knack for choosing the heart-breakers."

"I don't believe Decker's a heart-breaker." She studies me with a thoughtful look on her slender face. "In fact, I think he's extremely loyal to those he lets in."

"You don't know me." I slip my hands in my pockets and direct my gaze to the Manhattan skyline.

"I investigated the *Contender Sports* scandal," she says. "You stood by those kids, going as far as to pay their legal fees to ensure not only justice for what was done to them but financial compensation."

"It was the least I could do." My chest squeezes.

"You didn't have to, and you bankrupted yourself to make sure Adam Lamont never touches a child again." She stands and joins me at the window. "I'll be honest, Mr. Gabrielli. You passed the psych evaluation and medical exams, but you don't have the pedigree or noteworthy résumé I'm looking for. While you may be the most physically attractive applicant to ever walk through these doors, your looks aren't enough."

The verbal punch is enough to hitch my breath,

but I keep my lips pinned and my expression neutral. It's not like I wanted this job.

Except the idea of it is growing on me. Maybe it's the professional way she laid out the expectations or the guarantee that the relationship would be mutually enjoyed. Or maybe it's the most desperate incentive of all: Money.

"It's your integrity," she says, "that makes you extremely desirable as a candidate. Knowing you'll respect our code of conduct, ethics, and confidentiality carries more weight than a degree from Harvard."

My mouth dries, and my pulse speeds up. Is she offering me a job?

"Please." She gestures for me to take the seat beside Evan. "We have a lot to discuss."

I return to the chair and sit forward, elbows braced on my knees. "I haven't accepted the job."

"You will."

"I'm not—"

She holds up a hand. "You need income, and you're too smart to turn this down."

My nostrils flare. "I want to choose the woman."

"No. Client profiles are classified. You'll be introduced to one client only—the one we choose for you." She removes a three-page document from a folder on the desk and places it in front of me.

A quick glance confirms it's a contract, dated and filled out with my name. I don't touch it.

"If we broker this agreement," she says, "Infidelity will pay you twenty thousand dollars a month for a year. Will that sufficiently cover your outstanding attorney fees and dig you out of destitution?"

It's more than enough. More than I could ever

make slinging beer or mopping floors. It would give me a fresh start and maybe enough seed money to start up a new business venture.

"Yes," I say, with a thick layer of hope in my voice.

"Beyond the financial benefit, Infidelity will create opportunities for you. You'll dine with important constituents and socialize with powerful people who are always looking for entrepreneurial ideas to invest in."

Shit, I hadn't thought of that. And they won't know I'm a paid escort, since secrecy seems to be the most valuable service Infidelity offers.

"Your signature legally binds you to this agreement." She nods at the papers and reclines in the chair. "Sign the last page if you agree to a one-year relationship with the client you're assigned."

She walks through the physical abuse exception, how the agreement continues or terminates at the end of one year, and the mandatory monogamy—all of which Evan already explained.

"Will the one-year pledge of fidelity be a problem for you?" She sets a pen on the papers and locks her fingers together in front of her.

"No." I've never been in a committed relationship, but that's not the reason my stomach hardens with reluctance. "What if I'm not attracted to her? I don't want to sound like an asshole, but a woman can have sex when she's not into it. A man…" I share a look with Evan. "We have to be aroused to make it work."

"I promise," she says without a hint of embarrassment, "a virile man like yourself will have no problem performing."

"How the hell do you know?"

"I'm rarely wrong." She lifts her chin. "But on the small chance I am, there are pills for erectile problems."

Fuck that. Every molecule of male pride inside me cringes.

I can't do this.

Except it's only a year.

But what about my fucking dignity?

There won't be a shred of dignity left when I'm standing in line at a homeless shelter.

I slide the agreement toward me, read through it, and let myself consider the offer.

For the next hour, we go over the fine details, such as the possibility of me relocating to another city or state, potential traveling and fancy parties, living conditions, schedules, responsibilities, and media exposure.

If I do this, I'll be reduced to arm candy, the dude in a tux accompanying the big-shot politician or celebrity at social events. Can I live with that emasculating stigma for a year?

"Sign here, if you agree." She taps the paper. "And initial here and here."

I stare blankly at the agreement, my stomach a snarl of nerves.

What if I hate the woman? What if she's a total bitch? What if I find her nauseating and have to endure a year of her groping?

I picture Shelby at Blue Dixie with her hands on my dick and the cloying scent of her desperation fumigating my personal space day and night. Karen assured me I would enjoy the relationship, but if Infidelity wants me badly enough, she'll tell me anything to make me sign.

"Mr. Gabrielli, what's your answer?"

CHAPTER 5

Decker

What's my answer?

An obscene amount of money, enough prestige to potentially repair my reputation, and monogamous sex—that will be my incentive plan for the next year.

I pick up the pen and sign, trying to keep my hand from shaking through each stroke.

Evan grips my shoulder and squeezes. "You made the right decision."

I'm not so sure. I might not have sold my soul to the devil, but I just signed an agreement that sold my body to a woman I've never met.

After Evan and I shake hands and say goodbye, Karen sends me down the private elevator with her assistant to get photos taken for a passport and Infidelity's records. I fill out more forms in a conference room, providing details such as bank account information for direct deposits.

Two days ago I faced eviction and unemployment. Before that, I lived paycheck to paycheck, without electricity or frequent meals. Now I'll be earning a six-digit annual salary, living rent-free, and eating like a king. I feel wildly knocked off balance.

Karen's assistant pokes her blonde head into the conference room and smiles. "All finished?"

"Yep." I stand and head toward the door. "Do I

just wait for a call?"

With the interview check in my pocket, my next stop will be the phone store.

"Actually," she says, "Ms. Flores would like to speak to you before you go."

She escorts me back to level *I* and waves me into Karen's office, closing the door behind me.

Karen sits behind her desk, laptop closed, and expression expectant. "Take a seat."

I lower into the chair, narrowing my eyes. "Did something happen?"

"I have good news, Decker." Her grin is wide, her voice damn near breathless. "Normally, the medical evaluation and background check comes after the interview, but when Evan called me two days ago, I expedited the process."

My brows pulled together. "Because of my financial situation?"

"No. Let me reiterate that our clients pay a high price for a successful coupling. It can take weeks or longer to find the perfect match. We don't always have employees on hand that fit every profile. Sometimes we have to look outside of our existing staff to make these perfect pairings possible."

My heart pounds in my chest as I register the meaning of her words. "That's why you pushed so hard for me to sign. You hired me with a specific client already in mind. Why didn't you tell me?"

"There's an order to these things, Mr. Gabrielli. After your interview, I had to make some calls. Frankly, I didn't expect everything to line up as seamlessly as it did."

"Everything like what? You told me it could be a month before you matched me with someone." Fuck,

I'm not ready for this.

"I have a female client who requires a specific kind of companion. We don't have many male employees, which has made the process of filling her needs even more challenging. I've been searching for a profile like yours for a long time."

"What are her needs?" My palms slick with sweat. "Who is she?"

"I'm not authorized to say. What I can disclose is she flew into town this morning to meet you." Karen slides a square card across the desk. "You'll meet her tonight."

Waves of dread and excitement roll through my gut. If this woman doesn't live in town, that means I'll be moving. Doesn't matter in the scheme of things, but it's another big adjustment in the reckless whirlwind I've found myself in.

I glance at the embossed phone number on the card. "What's this?"

"If you need to report abuse, that's the number you call." She squares her shoulders. "The client received the same card."

A warning, probably one with more concern than usual, given my combat training. She knows I can defend myself against any man or woman and gave this to me as a reminder to keep myself in check.

"A car will pick you up at your residence at six tonight. Pack an overnight bag." She stands and offers her hand. "Congratulations, Mr. Gabrielli. Today is the first day of your one-year agreement. You're officially employed at Infidelity."

We shake hands, and I follow her out of the office, where she calls the private elevator. I try not to think about what comes with packing an overnight bag, but when the metal doors open, my nerves get the best of me.

"At least tell me what she looks like." I wink at her and flash my most charming smile. "Come on, Karen. Just a hint. Is she attractive? Old? Obese?"

Her expression gives nothing away, but there's a slight flush in her cheeks. "Good luck, Decker."

Fuck. I step into the elevator and catch the doors right before they close. "What do I wear?"

She gives me firm eye contact, her expression severe. "Be yourself."

CHAPTER 6

Decker

That night, I bounce my leg in the back of a limo as the tree-lined streets of the Village dissolve into the darkness behind me. When the driver picked me up in front of my apartment, he said nothing beyond a curt *Good evening, Mr. Gabrielli.* I could've made him walk the eight flights of stairs and meet me in my tiny studio, but I needed the frigid air to cool off my nervous energy.

It didn't help. My stomach's a mess, and I've chewed the hell out of my cheek. I don't know where the driver is taking me or why I'm alone in this pretentious car. Evidently, my soon-to-be *companion* is too busy or important to make the ride across town.

If I had to guess, my destination is somewhere private and secure, a place conducive to sex, like a hotel.

My overnight bag sits on the seat beside me, mocking me. Will I even need a change of clothes or will she keep me naked, on my knees, doing tongue exercises between her flabby old legs?

My gag reflex kicks in, and I drag a hand down my face, focusing my thoughts on anything but that.

I didn't leave much behind in my apartment. Just a couple boxes of clothes and combat sports gear. The rent's paid through the next two months thanks to the twenty-thousand-dollar advance that was deposited into my account a few hours ago.

Twenty grand, and I'm dressed like a hoodlum. My *Danzig* t-shirt should've been thrown out years ago, and my jeans are so worn the holes have holes. Faded converse, black leather jacket, and a studded belt—all of it says I don't give a shit. But Karen Flores said to be myself, and I wouldn't be caught dead shopping for clothes to impress a woman.

For the next fifteen minutes, I tap my fingers on the armrest and keep my thoughts on the end goal. Whoever this woman is, I'll charm the fuck out of her, keep her satisfied, and rub elbows with her wealthy network of friends. If I can drum up enough clout and money behind me, I might be able to open another combat sports school.

My chest expands with a rush of excitement. I have the experience to train all ages and skill levels. Raised in Brownsville, Brooklyn by a single mother, I learned how to scrap at a young age. It was run, fight, or die on those pot-holed streets, and I was never much of a runner. While my mom failed me in many ways, the year she put me in mixed martial arts lessons was everything. It gave me confidence, ambition, and focus when I needed it most.

Karen Flores was right about the *Contender Sports* business model. Children athletes are where the money's at. As it turned out, I discovered a passion in working with kids. I miss training with them, teaching them life skills, and watching them find their footing through tough adolescent years. While I might not be able to instruct another child again, maybe I can find an investor willing to fund a school for all ages. Maybe I'll find my passion again.

The limo motors along Central Park and stops in front of The Mark, a swanky hotel with a gold-trimmed overhang and a grand entrance. The driver hops out, but I don't wait for him to open my door. Grabbing the duffel bag, I step out and find another man in a suit, wearing a small receiver in his ear.

"Follow me, please." He leads me through the lobby, his shiny shoes moving silently across the black-and-white striped flooring.

Instead of pausing at the bank of elevators, he continues down a corridor and uses a badge to access an elevator tucked out of the way. When we step inside the lift, he swipes the card again to take us to the only upper floor available.

The other buttons lead to lower-level service floors and a parking garage, presumably a private garage. Why did he bring me in through the lobby? I guess the client isn't concerned about her association with me? Or maybe she's not as high-profile as I assumed? Maybe she slipped into the hotel through the private garage and no one knows she's here?

"Do you travel with her?" If I can coax this guy into conversation, I might be able to find out who she is or where she lives. "Or does she hire local security when she's in town?"

He stands sour-faced and statuesque like the Royal Guard at Buckingham Palace. So much for prying anything out of him. I might've tried harder, but the elevator slows to a stop.

The doors open to a contemporary lobby that's larger than my entire apartment. A winding staircase leads to a rooftop terrace, and several hallways trail off into more rooms and hallways. Dark wood floors, nickel lighting fixtures, and a profusion of white. Feels a little cold and a lot unwelcoming.

Footsteps approach from around the corner, and a man appears, wearing a perfect smile with sparkling white teeth.

"Decker Gabrielli." He shakes my hand. "I'm Reese Cromwell. Welcome." He flicks his wrist, gesturing me to follow him deeper into the suite. "How was the ride here?"

"Spacious." I clasp my hands behind my back and match his strides. "I don't mean to be rude, but who are you?"

Dressed in a collared shirt and designer jeans, he's ridiculously stylish and good-looking. Clean-shaven, physically fit, and not a blond hair out of place. If I had to guess, he's the same age as me, late-twenties, maybe younger.

"I run things around here." He walks through an elegant living room, passing multiple exterior doors that open to a private terrace with a prime view of the Upper East Side.

"What kinds of things?" I want to ask him what business she's in, what she looks like, and where the hell is she?

First, I need to know if he's clued in to the real reason I'm here. Karen said friends and family aren't privy to how the clients meet their companions. Does that confidentiality extend to the client's inner circle of employees?

I shrug off my jacket and toss it over a chair.

"I'm her personal assistant." Reese sits on one of two facing sofas and lifts a bottle of single malt whiskey from the coffee table. "I'm hesitant to use the term *assistant* here, because I manage every aspect of her personal life. Let's just say I manage her closet."

How many men does she keep in her closet? I pull in a deep breath and try to loosen my posture.

"Sit." He nods at the couch across from him. "Have a drink with me."

"Is she here?" I perch on the edge of the cushion and glance around, my gaze landing on the only closed door.

"We'll get to that. How about a toast?" He hands me a finger of whiskey and raises his own glass. "To a successful year with Infidelity."

So he knows. My insides twist, but I clink the glass with his and drink, relishing the burn in my throat. "Who is she?"

"I know you went through a thorough investigation and signed a one-year agreement." He slowly swirls his glass, watching the amber liquid swish round and round. "But I vet every person who enters her life, including her sexual partners. I need to be sure about you before I let you near her."

Why is he so protective? Is he one of her lovers, a close friend, or just a loyal employee? None of that narrows down her identity. She could be anyone, from a Supreme Court judge to a country music singer.

"Her pristine reputation is extremely important to her." He sets down the glass and laces his hands together between his spread legs. "She busts her ass to keep her public image respectable and her private life very *private*." His mouth crooks up. "You don't want to know how many men have sat exactly where you're sitting, interviewing to be a fuck buddy for a woman they've never met. Most are escorted out before learning who she is."

I sip the whiskey and stare at him.

"Money will buy the best-looking men in any city

or industry." He sits back and rests an ankle on his knee. "A lot of money buys their silence. The few men I've allowed into her bed did their job and kept their mouths shut. But you know what they didn't do?"

When he calls it a job, it sounds so damn shallow and mechanical. And what's this shit about allowing men in her bed? He handpicks her lovers? What kind of relationship does he have with this woman?

"I'm going to wager," I say, finishing off the whiskey, "they didn't make her happy."

He grins. "Exactly." He studies me for a moment, and his lips flatten. "I've succeeded in choosing companions who don't talk to the press, but I've failed in finding a compatible lover who suits her needs. So when she was referred to Infidelity, I jumped on it."

"That's just…" I'm dumbfounded by this conversation.

"What?"

"I don't know. I mean, most people go about this…organically. You know, crossing paths with someone and sparks fly, that kind of shit. Sounds like you're trying to force—"

"The world doesn't see her as a person, Decker. They see a name, a face. Her persona is an integral part of the worldview we're entrenched in. She's worshiped as much as she's judged, and every person she meets ultimately uses her for self-gain. All of this comes with the job, but it makes the organic way of dating impossible."

Reese Cromwell is a young, attractive guy with an obvious devotion toward this woman. There's no wedding ring on his finger, and I bet part of that is because he's married to this job. But I feel like there's something else going on. Does he love her? If that's the case, why the hell am I here?

"Are you fucking her?" I narrow my eyes.

"No." He makes a face that's difficult to interpret. Is that frustration? Disgust?

His boss is either ugly as hell or not interested in him. Given his winning looks, neither option bodes well for me.

He removes a document from the satchel sitting on the floor and hands it to me. The Infidelity logo embosses the top, followed by a list of hard limits. A name isn't printed anywhere on the page.

"These are *her* limits?" I ask.

"Yes."

I read through the thirty or so bullet points and deduce that she's unwilling to be on the receiving end of pain, bondage, or anything that puts her in a submissive position. It's identical to my own limits—the very ones I provided Infidelity. If she's as aggressive as I am in bed, I don't see how this is going to work.

"Are you good with her check list?" he asks.

Do I have a fucking choice?

"You already know I'm in this for the money." Impatience hardens my tone as I give the document back to him. "I'll respect her limits and do my best to make her happy for the contracted year."

Slouched on the couch, he taps a finger on his knee and scans my body up and down. "Given the extent at which Infidelity investigated you, I trust their word that you're a compatible companion for her. But there's one thing I suspect they didn't check." His eyes find mine. "Show me your cock."

Heat surges beneath my skin. "Go fuck yourself."

He straightens and rises to his feet, shoulders back and chest out. I mirror his pose, expecting a testosterone-fueled confrontation. Instead, a grin spreads across his face.

What the fuck? I get the feeling his request was less about the size of my cock and more about my reaction. Apparently, I passed the test, because he nods at the closed door on the far side of the room.

"Ready to meet her?" He wings up a perfectly trimmed eyebrow.

Yes. No. Christ, why is my heart slamming against my ribs? "After you."

He crosses the room and opens the door to the low murmur of a woman's voice—a husky radio voice that conjures images of lingerie, sensual curves, and red lips. I follow him into the bedroom and track the melodious sound to the glass wall that overlooks the terrace.

A slender woman with long blonde hair holds a phone to her ear and stares out at the blinking lights of the Manhattan skyline. She doesn't notice us, but when she shifts the phone to her other ear and tilts her head, her profile comes into full view. One of the most recognizable profiles on the planet.

My stomach drops. My pulse detonates, and my mouth goes dry.

Laynee Somerset.

She is the client I've been dreading?

This must be a joke. Who the hell would pay a guy like me twenty grand a month to fuck Laynee Somerset? I'm speechless and dizzy and…holy fucking shit, I hate to admit it, but I'm goddamn star-struck.

I meet Reese's eyes and clench my jaw. *You son of a bitch.*

He could've given me a clue, could've prepared me so that I wouldn't be standing here with my fucking eyes bugging out of my head.

Laynee Somerset isn't just an A-list movie star. She's the royalty of Hollywood. Her mother was a renowned actress in the wave of classic 1970s cult films, and her father was one of the most powerful film producers of all time. Both dead, they left behind a legacy in the form of the world's most beautiful and talented woman in show business.

I've seen most, if not all her movies, as well as countless interviews and magazine spreads. Not that I stalk her. Her glamorous face is everywhere.

She's also usually accompanied by her famous husband and fellow costar, Blake Harridan. But they can't be married. I specifically requested a single woman in my application. Christ, the thought of being used like a sex toy in a kinky celebrity marriage makes me want to hurl.

"No. I said no appearances. I'm leaving New York tomorrow and—" Laynee rests her forehead against the window and draws something across the glass with her finger. "I understand, but I'm not budging on this, Violet. No cameras. No fucking interviews. I swear to God, if I see the pap sniffing around—" She sighs. "Yeah, I trust you."

She shifts her weight from one foot to the other, her long legs and toned backside encased in tight yoga pants. A thin t-shirt hangs off one pale shoulder, and her golden hair falls in a sexy ruffled mess midway down her back.

I've only ever seen pictures of her in floor-length gowns, with her hair all done up, heavy makeup, and jewelry. The sight of her makeup-free and away from the flashing lights is more captivating than any airbrushed photo. My God, she's a stunning woman.

Graceful bone structure, perfect-sized ass, just enough curves to hold on to. She can't be real.

"No, I don't care." Her hand balls in a fist. "This is a personal trip, and I want to be in and out of the city without the circus." She turns, and her huge blue eyes lock on my face. "Listen, I need to go."

She hangs up and drags her gaze away to look at Reese. "The vultures are circling."

"You knew they would." He perches on the arm of a chair. "You haven't traveled in a while. They're hungry."

"Yeah, I know." She tosses the phone on the bed and walks toward me. "You must be Decker."

Fucking hell, she isn't wearing a bra. The pale green shirt may as well be transparent. Dusky nipples brush against the fabric, peaked with tight little buds.

I focus on her polished smile and hope to God my dick behaves. I should've worn looser jeans. "Forgive me. I'm…a little caught off guard here." I throw another glare at Reese and offer her my hand.

She doesn't shake it. Instead, she holds my palm in the cradle of hers and trails her fingers over the scars on my knuckles, exploring, caressing. I feel every stroke as if she were teasing the length of my cock.

"You're really young." She glances at Reese with grooves in her brow.

"So are you." I curl my fingers around hers, drawing her attention back to me.

"I'm forty." Her tone is as bitter as her smile. "That's a decade past old in my profession."

She's twelve years older than me? I've never been attracted to older women, but goddamn, her flawless beauty threatens to bring me to my knees.

"You're ageless," I say lamely.

"Hmm. Well…thank you." She releases my hand. "My beauty regime costs sixteen grand a month."

My head hurts at the thought of spending that kind of money on anything.

"Don't let her fool you." Perched on the chair behind her, Reese crosses his arms. "She's never done Botox. Never gone under the knife for any kind of cosmetic surgery. She's a rare natural gem among her peers."

She shakes her head, sharing an intimate smile with the other man.

My hands fist at my sides. I feel like an intruder in a private relationship. Doesn't matter who she is or what he means to her. I've been assigned to her, *to her bed,* and I don't share. For the next year, she'll be with me and no one else.

CHAPTER 7

Laynee

I keep a camera-ready smile arranged on my face while every nerve in my body shivers and heats. I've never in my life encountered a man this unbelievably gorgeous. It's astounding really, since I'm in the business of beautiful people. But it's not Decker's sex appeal that makes the hairs on my nape stand on end.

Reese knows my requirements in a companion, and I was very clear in my profile and conversations with Infidelity. *No overbearing alpha types.* I have enough people in my life ordering me around. I can't even sneeze without someone telling me how and when to do it.

And this man…this brick house of muscle and intimidation is already clenching his fists and staring at me like he owns me.

"Reese." I give my best friend a look that spurs him to stand from the chair. My smile tightens. "Can I speak to you in private?"

Decker glances between us, his brows dangerously dark over narrowed brown eyes. "Whatever you need to say to him, say it in front of me."

"That's not how this works." I give Decker my best glare.

He grabs the wooden desk chair, plants it in front

of the loveseat, and tosses the decorative pillows to the floor. "Sit."

My breath hitches with indignation. Where does this guy get off?

"Should I leave?" Reese takes a step toward the door.

"Yes," Decker barks at the same time I say, "Stay".

"Stay," I repeat in a stronger voice and direct my gaze to the loveseat, punctuating my order to Reese.

He steps over the scattered pillows and lowers onto the small sofa. With a flutter in my stomach, I sit beside him.

Decker perches on the wooden chair directly across from me, leaving less than a foot of space between our knees. I don't know what his problem is with Reese, but he scowls at the other man for an uncomfortable moment before turning his attention to me.

I need to get control of this situation, but I suck at confrontation. There's no way I'd be able to maintain my composure if I went head to head with this man. I'd rather grab the shackles out of my suitcase and restrain his hands to the armrests. It wouldn't shield me from the intensity of his eyes, but I'd feel a little safer knowing he couldn't physically hurt me.

It's a ridiculous fear. Infidelity assured me their employee screening process is unparalleled.

Leaning forward, Decker braces sinewy forearms on his thighs, and it's all I can do to maintain my practiced posture—spine straight, shoulders back, chin lifted.

"Your smile's faltering." He rubs his whiskered jaw, his expression thoughtful. "Do I make you nervous?"

"No," I say too quickly, unable to hold my mask in place. "Do I make *you* nervous?"

"Yes." He clasps his hands together between his bent legs. "Where's your husband?"

The question startles a laugh from me. "You mean Blake?" I study the confused look on his face. "You really don't know?"

His eyes darken.

"Do you not watch TV?" I should be offended, but the idea that he's clueless about celebrity gossip has a strangely wonderful effect on me.

"I don't own a TV." A muscle bounces in his cheek. "Are you married or not?"

"Divorced."

"It's been all over the news for the last month." Reese grunts. "Do you live under a rock?"

"Just this past month?" Decker doesn't take his eyes off me. "That's funny. Your assistant gave me the impression he's been selecting candidates for your bed for a while. Were you cheating on your husband?"

Reese jerks forward, but I put a hand out, staying him.

"I've never cheated. I divorced Blake two years ago." My chest pinches, but I don't let the pain show on my face. "Our publicist wanted us to keep the separation quiet until after the premier of *Cherry Springs*. Have you heard of—"

"I saw the movie," Decker says without inflection or emotion.

He stares at me so intently my skin flushes. Is he thinking about the graphic sex scenes between my on-screen character and Blake's? God, the filming and promotion of that movie was one of the most painful things I've ever done. Pretending to be blissfully in love with Blake—both on and off the screen—broke pieces inside me I'm not sure will ever heal.

I don't know why I feel the need to explain myself, but my mouth moves before I can stop myself. "I use body doubles. The nudity…the shots during the sex scenes that didn't show my face…that wasn't me."

He nods, and his shoulders seem to loosen. "Will you be filming more movies with your ex-husband?"

What a strange question, but since he's not in the business, I guess he wouldn't know how these things work.

"She won't be costarring with Blake again." Reese gives me a sympathetic smile. "Hollywood is all about pairing real-life couples on the big screen. But when a famous duo breaks up, it's ugly and scandalous and often career damaging." He squeezes my knee. "Laynee will bounce back. She always does."

Decker's gaze zooms in on Reese's hand until Reese removes his touch.

"Where do you live?" Decker cocks his head. "Beverly Hills?"

"Oh, uh… No." I curl my toes in the shaggy rug. "Savannah, actually. We're heading back in the morning."

"We?" Decker looks between Reese and me.

"The plan is to bring you with us." I meet his eyes. "I have a private plane, and it would be easier if—"

"Jesus." He leans back and rubs a hand over his head, mussing the tousled strands of his brown hair. "This is…"

"Fast?"

"That's one way to put it."

"The longer I stay in the city, the harder it is to slip under the radar."

Decker watches me with a blank expression.

"All it takes is one hotel employee." Reese bends forward, eyes tapered. "The server who delivers the meals, the maid, the technician monitoring the security cameras… Someone will violate their NDA and leak Laynee's location to the press. It's just a matter of time, probably hours, before paparazzi surround the hotel and make it a goddamn nightmare to leave."

"Okay." Decker rolls his lips in thought. Beautiful lips. Full, firm, kissable… "Tell me how I fit in to all of this."

"Well." My chest rises and falls with a sigh. "When the time is right, my publicist will create a buzz about my new *boyfriend.* A strategy that will promote the perception that I've moved on from Blake—"

"Perception?"

"I *have* moved on." I grind my teeth. "But in my world, perceptions are reality, and right now the perception is that I'm a scorned woman, hiding in my home and drowning myself in alcohol. *You* are the fix, but if I'm seen with you too soon, you'll be a rebound, and I'll be a whore. Timing is everything, and Violet knows how to navigate these things. She'll tell me when it's time to make public appearances together. Meanwhile…" I shrug. "You'll stay in my home and keep a low profile while I go out and prove to the world that I'm a happy independent woman."

Except I've been dragging my feet on that last part. I despise putting on a Hollywood smile for the cameras. I just want to be left alone. But at my age, it's hard to land leading roles in major motion pictures. I have to keep my name on top of the latest news.

Without a prominent, *desirable* public image, I'm out of work.

"So I'm here to solve your negative press." His hard brown eyes lock on me with caustic focus. "Explain how you see our private relationship playing out."

I share a look with Reese. When I agreed to hire Infidelity, the purpose was twofold. I need a stable companion to eventually accompany me at award shows and red-carpet appearances. But the deeper, more vulnerable reason is I ache for a lover I can trust.

I'm under no illusions that a dependable relationship will grow from a contractual agreement, but I'm tired of all the men shuffling in and out of my bedroom. I don't even have sex with most of them. They're too googly-eyed and overeager. I need a companion, not a fanboy. But more than that, I need a submissive man who won't walk all over me.

The fact that Decker Gabrielli isn't drooling at my feet and obsessing over my stardom is a breath of fresh air. But there isn't a servile bone in his rock-hard body.

"What's your relationship with him?" Decker nods at Reese.

"He's my personal assistant."

"Laynee." The reprimanding sound of my name on his lips makes me tremble.

"I don't like your tone." I set my jaw. "Questioning me isn't in your job description."

"Let me lay this out for you." He looks me directly in the eye. "I'll do whatever you ask in public. The fancy parties, the photo opportunities… I'll hold your arm and play the part of the smiling mindless escort. But in private, I will not be your whipping boy. Nor will I stand aside while you fuck other men and make a fool of me. *I* will be in your bed, and I do *not* share."

"What?" My blood boils. "I never said—"

"I'm not finished." He doesn't raise his voice, but he doesn't need to. His sheer presence demands compliance. "Whatever you're doing with him behind closed doors"—he thrusts a thumb at Reese—"it ends now."

My mouth hangs open.

"Tell me." He reclines in the chair and drapes his arms over the armrests. "How does Laynee Somerset entertain the men her assistant chooses for her?"

His condescending attitude makes me seethe from every pore in my body. Those men entertain me, not the other way around.

Christ, this is so outside my normal mode of operation. Yeah, Reese selects my companions and arranges the liaisons in hotel rooms like this one. Nine times out of ten, the guy is hard the instant he recognizes me. They get off on the idea of sharing a night with a celebrity. But I'm the one who controls the pleasure.

While Decker's question feels like a prompt for me to take the reins, it's just an illusion. I know his kind. I was married to a domineering piece of shit.

With a deep breath, I strengthen my spine and remind myself why he's here. "I restrain them."

"That so?" He arches a brow. "Show me."

CHAPTER 8

Laynee

With a belly full of butterflies, I rise to my feet like the empowered woman I strive to be and stride across the room. Holding my shoulders in perfect alignment, I keep my chin high and my gait slow and confident.

"Does your assistant always sit in on your play dates?" Decker reclines in the desk chair.

"I have a name, you know." Reese shifts to the edge of the loveseat.

"Yes." I dig the cuffs out of my suitcase. "He stays with me."

"Why?" Decker asks.

"It pleases me." I return to the sitting area, holding his gaze.

He plucks one of the cuffs from my hand and scrutinizes it with a smirk on his face.

"What?" I ask.

"I expected it to be lined with pink fur."

The muscles in my neck go taut. I had these shackles custom-made with thick black leather and heavy-duty metal buckles. They're my favorite cuffs.

"Are you mocking me?" I snatch it back.

"No. I approve." His smile seems genuine. "Carry on."

Arrgh. I'm holding the restraints, yet he's the one calling the shots? This is one of the million reasons I avoid men like him.

When I peek at Reese behind me, he rests a hand against his mouth. He thinks he's hiding his expression, but amusement gleams in his eyes. Damn him.

I turn back to Decker. "Arms on the armrests."

He sits taller in the chair and follows my order. His gaze kisses a trail of heat across my face, and when I bend down to buckle his wrist to the wooden arm, the warm whiskey scent of his breath saturates my senses. Each time my fingers graze his forearm—the sparse hair, smooth skin, and flexed muscle beneath—I fumble with the buckle.

"I like you like this." He reaches up with his free hand and brushes the hair from my face, tucking it behind my ear. "No makeup or fake smiles. Your natural beauty is devastating."

My heart stops, and it takes me a couple seconds to breathe again. "Your other hand."

He lowers his arm, and once he's securely buckled, I return to the loveseat and take him in.

Goddamn, he's hauntingly sexy. All lean muscle and self-confidence. His t-shirt stretches across defined pecs and a flat stomach. Low-waisted jeans give a peek of carved abs and pronounced indentions where his hips cut in. The dark shadow of whiskers and square jaw add to his masculine allure.

He's not bulky, yet he barely fits in that chair. It's his bearing, the way he holds himself. He radiates a don't-fuck-with-me vibe, one that any woman with a pulse would love to tame. I wouldn't mind feeling delicate and protected in his arms, but I've fallen for that fantasy before, and it ends in heartache.

Doesn't mean I can't enjoy him on my terms. My entire body shivers at the thought.

"You're staring." He doesn't move, doesn't even twist his wrists in the cuffs.

"I like you like this." I echo his words with a playful smile. "Bound and at my mercy."

"So bondage is your thing. The other guys…" His jaw twitches. "They're into this shit?"

I've restrained dozens of men, and it's always the same. They squirm and sweat with hard-ons tenting their pants. In the end, they all come.

"They get their night with a celebrity." I shrug. "And I get to do what pleases me. It's mutually beneficial."

Except the bulge in Decker's jeans isn't hard. He's either completely unaffected by this or damn good at controlling his responses.

"And what is that?" he asks. "What pleases you?"

I lift a bare foot and press my toes against his inner thigh, spreading his legs wider. He doesn't fight me, but his gaze darts to Reese.

Therein lies Decker's hard limits. I memorized his profile, the details surrounding the tragedy that destroyed his company, his financial issues, and his hard limits. *No sex with men. Nothing breaches his ass.* I won't cross his boundaries, but I will push against them.

"I like to watch." Just thinking about watching two men go at it makes my nipples harden and my panties wet.

He glances at my chest and grunts a sound of disbelief. "My hands are tied, sweetheart. Since I can't stroke my dick for you, what exactly are you going to watch?" He drags his gaze to Reese, and an uneasy smile seizes the corner of his mouth. "Ah."

I nod at Reese without looking away from the

man making my pussy throb. It's a guarantee Decker will fight this. My hands tremble with nerves even as wet heat gathers between my legs.

Reese kneels before him and reaches for the button on Decker's fly. If Decker's breathing speeds up, it's not noticeable. He doesn't move a muscle.

"Tell me what this is, Laynee." His voice is smoke and shrapnel.

"I like to watch Reese suck men off." My pulse races. "He's going to pull you out and wrap his mouth around you."

"No," Decker says calmly. "Not going to happen."

Reese slides down the zipper on Decker's jeans, and the sound echoes through the room.

Decker's fingers twitch on the armrest. "What do you get out of this?" His glare is bone-chilling.

I suck in a hungry breath. "Exactly what you'd get from watching two beautiful women go down on each other. It's hot, Decker."

Reese grips Decker's waistband to shimmy the jeans and briefs down his hips.

"I wouldn't do that." Decker remains still as a statue, his tone unnervingly composed.

When Reese glances back at me with hooded eyes, I don't have to look at his groin to know he's hard. I see that heated expression whenever he fucks a woman or man in front of me. He's such a dirty exhibitionist, and that totally works for me.

I give him a chin nod. *Keep going.*

"I'm the client, Decker." I lean back on the couch and tuck my legs beneath me, settling in. "You're paid to please me, and this is what I want."

The sight of Reese on his knees with his head

over Decker's lap produces mini-spasms between my legs. Where Reese is boyishly handsome and safe, Decker is potently mature and gorgeous and scary as hell. Just imagining his cock in Reese's mouth heats my skin from the inside out. If I knew Decker better, if I trusted him, I'd consider sucking him myself.

He stares down at the top of Reese's head, and something seems to settle over him, a calmness that makes my scalp tingle. Reese pulls on Decker's waistband, and intuition sends me lurching forward. Too late.

The chair flies up behind Decker, and his knees drop to the floor, taking Reese with him. In one fluid movement, Decker hooks a leg around Reese's throat, maneuvering him into a chokehold that has him writhing on his back and clawing at Decker's thigh.

"Let him go!" I launch at Decker, yanking on his leg, unable to move him.

"Tap the floor if we have an understanding." Decker suspends the chair behind his back, his wrists still shackled to the armrests.

"You're hurting him!" My voice shrills, and my heartbeat roars in my ears. "Release him right now!"

Reese's mouth gapes soundlessly, eyes bulging, and face bright red as he slams his palm on the floor, tapping frantically.

In the next breath, Decker stands and takes a step back, holding the chair behind him.

Reese grabs his throat and rolls to his side, coughing.

I clutch his shoulders and run my hands through his hair, my stomach roiling with guilt. "I'm so sorry."

"I'm fine. It's fine." He laughs and falls to his back on the floor. "We read his background, Laynee.

Are you really surprised?"

Decker might've been a trained fighter, but he seemed so calm in the restraints. *Right up until Reese tried to blow him.*

Turning, I find Decker sitting in the chair, arms still shackled to the armrests and legs stretched out in front of him. Completely unruffled with his zipper open and black briefs peering through.

Arrogant motherfucker. This is exactly why I don't mess around with men like him. I provoked him. I know this, but abusers don't always need a reason to attack. If I let this man into my house, I'll wake up in a few months in the same position as before—hiding bruises and digging myself out of self-hatred.

"I don't give a shit about the agreement." I close the distance, hands shaking as I remove the cuffs. "Clearly, Infidelity doesn't know the first thing about compatibility." I toss the shackles. "Get out."

He rubs his wrists, and half of his mouth lifts in a smile. "If I got a dollar every time someone told me to do that…"

"I mean it. I want you gone. This…" I wave a hand, indicating his pompous attitude. "This isn't what I paid for."

Rising from the chair, he prowls toward me.

I back up. "What are you doing?" I continue back-stepping, my heart rate jolting beneath that look in his eyes. "I told you to leave."

With a long stride, he reaches me, throws me over his shoulder, and carries me to the bed.

"Put me down!" I crane my neck and find Reese retreating from the room. "Reese!"

He closes the door, shutting me in with this…this caveman! Oh my God, I'm going to kill him. Both of them.

"Decker—"

He dumps me unceremoniously on the bed. My pulse explodes, and before I can scramble away, he's on top of me, his chest pressing against mine and his hands pinning my arms above my head.

"Get off me!" I buck beneath him, kicking and writhing and wearing myself out.

"God, you're feisty." He traps my legs with the weight of his.

My breath wheezes out of control, and black spots dot my vision. *FuckFuckFuck.* I'm going to have a panic attack.

"Shh." He shifts my wrists to one hand and gently brushes the hair from my face. "I'm not going to hurt you."

I've heard that before. So many fucking times. Sharp pain stabs through my chest and invigorates my struggling. I can't do this. Not again. "I just watched you choke—"

"Reese touched me without permission. I neutralized him."

"You're touching…me…" *No air. Can't breathe.* I twist my wrists in the manacle of his hand. "Let go!"

"Breathe, Laynee." He releases my arms and braces his upper body on an elbow.

The space he put between our chests helps, but he's still here, all around me, twice my size, and a hundred times my strength. He's too much, too strong, clouding my senses with his hard body and masculine scent. I can't think when he's this close, watching me with those intelligent eyes.

"Another breath." He strokes my hair, waiting until I obey. "Good girl. Now another."

My breathing evens out, but I'm still angry and scared shitless. "Why are you still here?"

"Infidelity is paying me to be your companion. I signed a one-year agreement."

"It was a mistake. You can go. I'll call them and fix it."

"I don't think so." He regards me with so much intensity I turn my head.

My bones feel heavy, and my insides clench and cramp. I hate that he scares me this much. I hate that I escape these situations only to end up right where I started. I should've told Decker to leave the moment he prowled into the room. But beautiful dominant men are my weakness. I'm fucking weak.

With a gentle grip on my jaw, he forces my eyes back to his. "When you restrain those men and watch them with Reese, what happens after? Do you fuck them?"

"That's none of your business."

"Communication is the only way this will work." He searches my eyes, probing, seeing too much. "I signed an NDA and a dozen other forms. I won't hurt you physically, emotionally, or with any of the information you give me. You have my word."

I draw in a shredded breath. "I fuck them…sometimes."

"Define *sometimes.*"

"I don't know." I give him a shrug and play it off.

He's going to figure out something's wrong with me, and for whatever reason, I don't want him to think less of me.

"Give me an estimate," he says. "Do you fuck them fifty-percent of the time? Once a week? Every other—"

"Twice." *Why did I just admit that?*

"Twice a week?" Not a hint of judgment in his tone.

I shake my head. "Twice in two years."

His breath catches, and something sparks in his eyes before he closes them.

"Thank you." When his lashes lift, his gaze roams my face, his expression contemplative. "Since we're leaving in the morning—"

"*I'm* leaving tomorrow. You're—"

He presses a finger against my lips. "I need to take care of something before we go." He removes his hand to glance at his watch. "I'll do that tonight."

"I told you—"

"I won't be gone long." He looks around the room. "Is this where we're sleeping?"

"This is *my* room." The thought of sharing a bed with him skyrockets my pulse. "Your room's on the other side of the penthouse."

"Tonight, we're just sharing a bed." He cups my jaw, his eyes as steely as his voice. "Nothing more."

He fists my hair and angles my head back, the possessive hold causing my objection to come out as a squeak of noise. I peer up at him, breathless, and find him staring at my mouth. Is he going to kiss me? Do I want him to?

No. Definitely not.

My heart flutters. My lips feel tingly, hyper-sensitive, and swollen, and he hasn't even lowered his head.

When he leans back instead of closing the distance, every cell in my body protests. This isn't good. He captivates me, terrifies me, and turns my brain into a rattletrap of conflicting wants. No man should have this much power over a woman.

He claimed he's still here because of the agreement, but why did he sign the damn thing in the first place? Money? Power? Sex? Isn't that what every man wants?

They all want something from me. They take, take, take, because why not? I'm rich and famous and don't have feelings. They're all smiles and compliments and promises...right before they stab me in the back. Literally.

"I can't do this." I push at his chest. "I don't do sleepovers. Not with anyone."

"I don't either, but this is going to be a venture in exceptions." He releases me, slides off the bed, and stalks toward the door.

I scramble after him. "I'm calling Infidelity and canceling the agreement."

"Okay." He tosses a cocky smirk over his shoulder. "You'll call Ms. Flores. She'll tell you you're shit out of luck. You'll spend the rest of the night lamenting Infidelity. Then I'll come back, slip into bed behind you, and hold you close. You'll put up a good fight, but you'll eventually wriggle that ass against me." A wolfish grin. "Because you find me irresistible."

"Oh my God, you have such a huge head."

"I know, and you want it thrusting inside you. But I insist we get to know each other first." He opens the door. "See you in a couple hours."

"Don't you dare come ba—"

The door shuts, leaving me aroused and fuming and completely off-kilter. What the hell just happened?

I flex and loosen my hands. He might be right about some things, but I'm still in control here. He'll be running the other way by the end of the night.

CHAPTER 9

Decker

I leave the beautiful Miss Somerset shaken—just enough to keep her guessing—and stroll through the empty living room with a heady surge of energy.

Laynee's the last person I expected, and while she might be a frustrating pain in the ass with a closet full of baggage, I'm goddamn giddy over the thought of sparring with her again.

Tonight.

In her bed.

I meant it when I said I don't do sleepovers. Most of my hookups end with the woman begging me to stay as I pry her off my body and make my escape. Laynee might be gorgeous and wealthy, but I can find women like that all over the city, and I don't have to do shit to spark their interest. The thing is I *want* to work for it, and Laynee's thrown down the gauntlet. The faster she retreats, the harder I'm going to chase.

Grabbing my jacket from the chair in the sitting room, I wander down a hallway and find Reese in the kitchen. Bent over the island, he's engrossed by his phone.

"Let's go." I nod in the direction of the elevator.

"Go?" He straightens. "Where?"

"I need to see a guy. Just a quick trip to the Village and back."

"Oh. Okay." He glances down the hall toward the master suite, brows scrunching. "I need to…uh…"

"Run along and ask permission. I'll meet you at the elevator."

Shrugging on my jacket, I find my way out. The short walk leads me past two…four…five security guards. Some are loitering. Others are coming and going. When I reach the front lobby of the penthouse, another guard sits in a chair beside the card reader for the lift.

"I need a keycard to leave?" I ask.

"Yes, Sir." He pulls one out of his pocket and swipes it over the reader.

"How many bodyguards are with her on this trip?"

"I'm not authorized—"

"Ten," Reese says behind me just as the elevator opens.

"Jesus." I follow him inside the lift. "Why so many?"

"She's famous." His tone is casual, but there's more to it.

Before I can ask, he presses the button for the private garage—exactly where I don't want to go.

"We're taking the subway." I reach for the button labeled *Lobby*.

"No way." He blocks me from pressing it. "I'm not usually recognized, but it's better to err on the side of discreet."

"A limo isn't discreet."

"We're taking her car."

I follow him into the garage, where a black SUV waits a few feet away. The driver—an older woman wearing a navy pants suit—opens the rear door. I give her the address of a Greenwich Village restaurant and slide into the backseat after Reese.

"Why am I coming with you?" He latches his seatbelt and watches me do the same.

"Three reasons." I rest an elbow on the window ledge as the SUV exits the garage.

"Those are?"

I point my chin at the driver sitting within earshot and raise a brow at Reese.

"She's one of our trusted employees," he says. "Rachel, meet Decker. Decker, Rachel."

She raises a hand in greeting and navigates the SUV into the cluster of traffic.

"I brought you along as an insurance policy." I cast him a pointed look. "Laynee won't leave without you."

"Okay." He draws out the word. "But she can't exactly skip town in a couple hours. It takes time to prep the plane and assemble her entourage."

"I think she can do anything she wants when she's pissed."

"She's pretty pissed." He nods thoughtfully. "What's the second reason?"

"Crisis prevention. I have no idea how to handle a reporter. If my association with her was leaked while I was in the hotel, I'm not prepared to deal with that. Screwing up her public image is the last thing I want."

"That's cool of you." He taps his fingers on his leg. "Really cool actually. I'm impressed."

He stares at me with more admiration than I'm comfortable with, especially after he just tried to go down on me.

"The third reason you're tagging along…" I shift to face him. "We need to have a conversation."

"I figured."

"You're bi-sexual."

He gapes at me like he can't believe I said that.

"Don't fuck with me." A scowl twists my lips. "You went after my dick."

"I know. I was there," he deadpans. "It's just…most guys assume I'm gay."

I blow out a sharp breath. "I saw the way you look at her. Do you love her?"

"Yes. But it's not what you think."

"Then explain it." My jaw flexes with impatience.

"We tried to be…exclusive."

"You fucked her?" My voice whips through the confined space.

"We didn't get that far. Look, it's hard to explain. Just know that she and I… We're not compatible in that way."

"I need more than that."

"It's better if you figure it out yourself."

Fucking games. I despise them.

From what I gathered during my brief introduction to Laynee Somerset, she has intimacy issues. She restrains men but doesn't fuck them. She has some kind of sexual arrangement with Reese, but they're not compatible in bed. She wants me, but it's clear she's trying to talk herself into hating me. Why? Because I wouldn't let Reese suck my dick? I think it goes way deeper than that, and I intend to find out.

The SUV motors down Seventh Avenue, filling the windows with the bright lights of commercial signs and passing cars. I've never traveled outside of the New York-New Jersey area and can't wrap my mind around living somewhere else. Especially not Savannah. What the hell will I do there?

Laynee. That's what I'll do.

"You know," Reese says, "she probably called Karen Flores the instant you left."

"Yep."

"You don't seem concerned."

"The only way out of this agreement is physical abuse."

He rubs his throat, and I shake my head. Putting him in a chokehold was self-defense, not assault. But even if I physically harmed him, it wouldn't void the agreement. Laynee's the client, not him.

"Word of advice." I harden my eyes. "Don't touch me, and I won't touch you."

"Got it."

"Do you? Because I feel like this is going to be an issue."

"No, it's—"

"You're attracted to me."

He clears his throat and stares out the side window, hiding his expression. "Yes."

I try to keep the irritation out of my tone. "You want to fuck me?"

"I…um…"

"We're going to have this conversation while you're looking at me."

A few seconds pass before he shifts his eyes to mine and says quietly, "I prefer…"

"Speak up."

"I prefer it the other way around. *You* fucking *me*."

My stomach clenches. "Is that how it works with the others you bring to her?"

"I fuck them." He slides his palms over his jean-clad thighs and holds my gaze. "She likes to watch."

"Are they bi-sexual?"

"Not always." The corner of his mouth lifts. "You'd be surprised what a straight man will do when Laynee Somerset is in the room."

The notion makes my stomach hurt. I don't care who the woman is. I would never be able to get it up for a dude.

"I don't fuck men." I say sternly. "And no one fucks me. You and I can be friends, but that's it. Are we clear?"

"I understand." He chews on a fingernail.

"Same goes for Laynee. No more voyeuristic, partner-sharing…whatever you two dabble in. Going forward, your relationship with her is strictly platonic."

He turns toward the window and rests a fist against his mouth. The SUV travels several blocks, and the Village comes into view. We're almost there, but the silence between us is heavy, suggesting the conversation isn't over.

"Say what's on your mind." I stare out the windshield, watching him stir in my periphery.

"She can be difficult." He fidgets with the zipper on his wool coat.

"I noticed."

"I don't think she likes you."

"Oh, she likes me. She just doesn't want to like me."

"She's not going to make it easy for you." He tips his head toward me.

"I'm counting on that."

We lock eyes, and a smile plays on the corner of his mouth. I don't smile back, but my entire body vibrates with excitement. If Laynee's as headstrong as she seems, I might've finally met my match.

Our destination—a French-style *tapas* restaurant—emerges on the left, and Rachel pulls to a stop in the small over-packed parking lot.

"We'll be fifteen…twenty minutes," I tell her. "Good luck finding a place to park."

"I'll circle around until you come out." She unlocks the doors.

Reese follows me out and jogs after me toward the rear entrance of the restaurant. "What are we doing here?"

"My buddy waits tables on the night shift." I veer onto the sidewalk and slip my hands into the pockets of my jacket to ward off the chilly air. "Just checking in with him before I leave town."

The stench of a nearby dumpster wafts through the dark alley behind the restaurant. There's no one around, and the back door is closed. I pull on the handle. Locked.

Huddling closer to the building, I shiver against the bitter wind. "Won't be long. Someone will step out for a smoke break."

"Why don't we use the front entrance?" Reese leans a shoulder on the brick wall beside me, his breaths forming plumes of white vapor.

"The hostess won't be happy to see me." I cringe at the memory of my last encounter with Apryl.

"Why am I not surprised?" He smirks.

"That's bullshit. I always leave behind a satisfied smile."

"Until they find out there won't be seconds?"

"On a good night, there's definitely seconds." I grin. "And thirds—"

The door swings open, and I turn to find the last person I want to see.

"You." Apryl shoves a hand through her short black hair, her face contorting into the pixie version of a roid rage. "What the fuck are you doing here?"

"Calm down. I just need—"

"No." She throws the bag of trash she carried out, her voice spiking from pissed off to psychotic. "If you think I'll take you back, you can go fuck yourself."

Jesus Christ, she thinks I'm here for her? The woman is a complete and utter nightmare. Why I ever thought it was a good idea to stick my dick in her is beyond me. Granted I was drunk, but goddamn, I should've known better.

Reese chews on his lip, his eyes glimmering in the moonlight.

"Apryl." I raise my hands in a placating gesture. "I'm here to see Dan."

"You're a fucking asshole, you know that?" She storms toward me, fists balled at her sides. "Why aren't you returning my texts?"

Where do I begin? The sex was sloppy. She's clingy and unhinged, and I have no idea how she got my number. I blocked her messages after the first twenty-four hours. That was *two months* ago.

"We're not doing this." I sidestep her, easily evading her pathetic punch. "I need you to go get Dan."

I'd get him myself, but she'll follow me in and make a horrendous scene.

"I hate you." She swings again.

This time I let her knuckles connect with my chest. Maybe she'll wear herself out.

"You're such a womanizing manwhore." She goes ballistic, slapping my torso and spitting a string of insults. "I know you fucked Cassie and Iliza and God knows who else, you fucking slut."

When I visit Dan at work, sometimes I go home with a waitress…or two. I'm a horny *single* guy, and I don't have to explain myself to anyone. Especially not to this deranged woman.

I stand still and let her fists bounce off my body like a petulant fly. Doesn't take long before her breaths become labored, and her slaps slide into heavy caresses.

"I miss you, dammit." Her forehead falls to my chest. "You broke my heart."

"We had sex *one time*." I wince against a bony punch in the ribs and gently push her away. "Ten minutes in a bar bathroom, Apryl. It wasn't your heart I was fucking."

"Don't minimize my emotions." She stabs a finger at her chest. "What I feel is *real!*"

I catch Reese's grin out of the corner of my eye and struggle to keep a straight face. It really is kind of funny…in a sad, mentally unstable way.

"Why, Decker?" She flings herself at me, arms wrapping around my waist and face buried against my chest. "You just threw me away like it meant nothing."

My hands hover in the air above her as she hangs on my body. I should tell her the truth—she lost her appeal the moment she went from cute to batshit obsessive—but I'm not that vicious. I want her gone, not emotionally destroyed. So I opt for an easy out.

"My grandma died," I say in a quiet tone.

"What?" She lifts her head and searches my eyes. "How?"

"She was…" I say the first thing that pops into my head. "Beaten." I slide a hand down her back, as if seeking solace. "Someone broke into her house and beat her with a baseball bat." *I'm going to hell.*

"Oh my God. I had no idea." Just like that, her

hysteria evaporates, replaced with soft petting hands and adoring eyes. "I'm so sorry, Decker."

Reese folds his arms across his chest and does a piss poor job of hiding his grin.

Laugh it up, asshole.

"I have to leave town for a while." I grip her shoulders and put space between us.

"For the funeral?" She clutches my wrists. "I can go with you. You know, if you need" – a vixenish smile – "comforting."

My stomach turns. "I'll be fine. Can you go get Dan for me?"

"Yes, of course." She strokes my chest. "When you get back… Well, you have my number."

I probably shouldn't tell her I deleted it. "I'm in a hurry, Apryl."

She moves in for a kiss, and I turn my head right before her lips graze my jaw.

"Okay, I'll just…" She steps back. "I'll be waiting for your call."

I give her a wave. *Keep walking. There you go. Don't forget to take your meds.* The door closes behind her, and I blow out a breath. *Fuck.*

"What was that?" Reese huffs a laugh.

"A mistake."

"Which part?"

"All of it."

"I'm embarrassed for you."

I drop my head back and close my eyes.

"You have any more mistakes following you around?" he asks.

"We're not talking about this."

"I mean, she didn't even notice me standing here. Those crazy eyes were all for you."

"Enjoying yourself?"

"Tremendously."

A few seconds later, Dan opens the door, wearing the requisite server uniform. The sleeves of his button-up are rolled to the elbows, and the end of his necktie is tucked beneath an apron.

"A dead grandma, dude?" He hugs himself, hunching against a biting gust of wind. "Do you even have a grandma?"

"Not that I know of."

"I was going to warn you away from Apryl." He shakes his head, grinning. "Gorgeous girl. Tight pussy. But clingy as a chronic STD."

"Yeah, thanks for the heads up." I glower at him.

"I've been trying to call you the last couple days." He gives Reese a cursory glance and turns back to me. "Where've you been?"

"Lost my job. Phone was shut off, but it's back on now. Long story. Anyway, I'm heading out of town for a while."

"What? Why?"

I've known this guy for years and don't want to lie to him. He'll see photos of me with Laynee eventually, but until then, I'm bound by an NDA. So I keep my answer vague.

"I met someone."

He looks at Reese, who leans against the building wearing an unreadable expression.

"Not him," I say. "Well, yeah, I met him recently." I do quick introductions. "Reese isn't the reason I'm leaving."

"So what's the deal?" Dan rubs a hand over his shaggy blond hair, studying my face. "Are you in trouble?"

"Nothing like that. This is a good thing, man. I just need you to trust me."

"Yeah, okay. How long will you be gone?"

"A year."

"No shit? That sounds serious."

"I'm keeping my apartment." I pull a key from my pocket and place it in his hand. "It's yours for the next year. Rent-free."

"No, I…" He stares at the key and curls his fingers around it. "I thought you were behind on the rent."

"Rent and utilities are taken care of. Don't ask questions, Dan. Just say thank you and move in."

"I can't. This is too much." He tries to give the key back.

I shove my hands in the pockets of my jacket. "Where're you sleeping this week?"

His eyes cut to Reese and return to me. "Here and there."

"Homeless shelter?"

"I'm working things out, picking up extra shifts, and—"

"Now you have one less thing to worry about. You'd do the same for me." I pull him in for a one-armed hug and step back. "I'll call you when I'm settled. We good?"

He stares at the ground, slips the key into his pocket, and nods. "I don't know how to thank you, Decker."

"Get your son back, yeah?"

"Yeah."

I clap him on the back and walk toward the parking lot. Reese falls in step beside me, hands clasped behind him, and I welcome his silence.

We climb into the SUV and head back to the Upper East Side before he asks, "What's his story?"

"His wife cheated on him, wiped out his bank account, and took his kid. The little money he earns is wrapped up in a hellacious custody battle. A battle he'll never win if he doesn't have a place to live."

"Damn." He watches the traffic flickering by, head tilted against the window. "Who knew you were a softy?"

"If I was a softy, I would've let him move in with me months ago. Sharing a studio apartment with another guy exceeds my generosity."

"That would exceed anyone's generosity."

I've felt bad about Dan's situation for a long time. Giving him a place to live is a huge weight off my shoulders.

Pay it forward. I smile at Evan's motto. Maybe he's on to something.

When we reach the penthouse, I make my way toward the master suite.

"Your room is back there." Reese chases after me. "Where are you going?"

"Goodnight, Reese." I approach the closed door.

With a soundless twist of the handle, I confirm it's locked. From my wallet, I remove the credit-card-sized lock pick set.

"What're you doing?" Reese whispers behind me.

I slide one of the picks into the keyhole, and it unlocks with a *click*.

"Why are you carrying a lock pick set in your wallet?" He glares at me.

I've had it since I owned my store fronts. Didn't want to chance getting locked out.

"I wouldn't go in there," Reese says. "This is a

bad idea."

I open the door and shut it behind me, locking Reese out. As my eyes adjust to the shadows, I trace the path of moonlight from the windows to the bed and find Laynee kneeling on the mattress.

"Don't come any closer." With her arms stretched out in front of her, she points a handgun at my chest.

Startled, I plant my feet on the floor, hands at my sides, and narrow my eyes. I can't tell if she's bluffing. Is the weapon even loaded?

Her finger moves to the trigger, and my pulse quickens.

"Lower the gun, Laynee." I keep my voice quiet yet stern. "Odds are you'll send a bullet through the wall and hit your assistant in the next room."

"I learned how to shoot on the set of *Angel of Fear*. Did you see that movie? That wasn't special effects. I'm a damn good shot."

I believe her, and fuck if my cock doesn't harden. Seeing her in cotton panties, a tiny tank-top, and confidently aiming a gun sets my body on fire. I want her more than I've wanted anyone or anything in a long fucking time.

"I take it your conversation with Infidelity didn't go well." I resist the urge to adjust my boner.

"I'm stuck with you, but the agreement doesn't require you to be in my bed. We'll stick to the script." She shifts toward the end of the mattress on her knees, training the gun on my torso. "You'll be my boyfriend in public only. No sex. No touching when the cameras aren't around."

"Do you believe your own bullshit?" I laugh. "No sex for a year? Do I look like a goddamn monk?"

She sucks in a sharp breath. "You signed an

agreement to be monogamous."

"Monogamous. Not celibate." I take a cautious step toward her. "I enjoy sex, Laynee. I intend to enjoy it every day and in every way with my *companion*."

"Not another step." She stiffens her arms, the gun steady in her hands.

"Shooting me might get you out of the agreement, but the best publicist in the business can't explain away a dead body in your hotel room."

"Don't do this." The plea cracking her voice feels like a fist in my chest.

"All right." Backing down goes against every aggressive cell in my body, but I'm pushing too hard, too soon. "I'll give you tonight to—"

"You don't get to—"

"—sleep alone. In Savannah, we do this my way."

I slip out of the room, without giving her a chance to argue. Bracing my arms on the door frame, I listen for her muffled footsteps on the other side. When the lock clicks, I turn toward the sitting room.

As expected, Reese perches on the couch, wearing a smug expression. "Told you not to go in there."

"She travels with ten bodyguards. Why does she need a gun?"

"Makes her feel safer." He stands and heads down the hall toward the kitchen.

"Safe from what?" I follow on his heels, my mind racing in a million directions. "Does she have a stalker?"

"Several." He opens the fridge and pulls out a dark beer. "Want one?"

"No. Have they breached security? Are they threatening her life?"

"No one gets past her security." He pulls a long

draw from the beer, watching my face turn rigid with tension. "Don't get all worked up about this, Decker. There will always be stalkers. We find one, and a new one pops up. It's just the way it is."

"Unacceptable." I thrust a finger toward the master suite. "If she's scared enough to travel with a gun, her guards aren't doing their jobs."

His gaze drops to the floor.

"There's something else." My nostrils flare. "What is it?"

His silence incenses me. There's so much I don't know about this woman, and I'm about to be deeply entangled in her life. Is there a connection between her intimacy issues and her need to sleep with a gun?

"Did someone hurt her?" I flex my hands.

A muscle jumps in his cheek, and he tries to hide the reflex behind a swallow of beer.

"Who?" I crowd him, putting my face in his. "The ex-husband?"

He presses his back against the fridge, glaring at me. "You need to talk to her about this."

"I intend to." *When she's not aiming a gun at my chest.* "Take me to her head of security."

CHAPTER 10

Laynee

Decker's been quiet since we left New York. But where he's distant with words, he's invasive in the sheer intensity of his eyes. He watches me from the back of my plane, while talking to my security detail on the flight to Savannah. He stares at me in the Range Rover as we ride to my home.

Now I feel his gaze caressing the ass of my jeans as I lead him up the stairs to the bedrooms.

Keeping my eyes forward, I cross the second-floor landing with a steady *click-click-click* of my heels. "Make arrangements with Reese to have your things brought here from New York."

"That's not necessary." His deep voice rumbles closer than I expected.

Whirling around, I find him inches away and stumble back. "What about all your clothes and personal things?"

"Everything I need is here." He backs me against the wall without touching me. How the fuck does he do that?

I crane my neck, searching for Reese. He was behind us a second ago. Dammit, where did he go?

The prickly chill of fear rises up the back of my neck. I told Reese on the flight home not to leave me alone with this man.

I angle my chin in the direction of the guest rooms. "Your room is—"

"Your room." Decker drops his duffel bag on the floor and braces his arms on the wall above my head.

As he leans in, no part of him comes in contact with me, but I feel him…everywhere. The warmth of his breath, the potency of his effusive gaze, and the lazy confidence radiating from his posture—all of it is predatory, sexual, and dangerous.

"Step back." I lock down the urge to scream for Reese, but I can't control my runaway breaths or the thunder of my heart.

He takes in my heaving chest, lingers on my throat, and returns to my eyes. "Focus on my voice, Laynee. Breathe when I breathe. In. Out…"

With each silken word, he sets a hypnotic pace. I concentrate on his timbre and the movement of his lips, breathing when he breathes. The heat emitting from his muscled body permeates my blouse and seeps into my skin, soothing me as much as it confuses me. For a fuzzy moment, I almost forget why I panicked.

"Do you have this reaction to every man you meet?" he asks quietly.

My eyes lock on the burnish of his. He's so close I can see the gold flecks pulsing in the striations of his brown irises. I blink and look down, incidentally zooming in on his lickable mouth.

"Laynee?"

Shit, he asked me a question, and I don't know how to answer it. Submissive men don't scare me. But men like Decker? I fucking freeze up.

His scowl tells me my reaction annoys him. Well, fuck him, because it annoys me, too. I've spent a fortune on therapy, and while I've made huge progress over the years, I still hyperventilate in the presence of dominant personalities.

"I'll give you a pass on that question for now." He lowers an arm, allowing me a sliver of space to breathe. "Tell me about your home."

Grateful for the reprieve, I stand taller and compose myself. "Reese can give you a tour—"

"I don't want a tour. I want you to tell me what this place means to you."

He's probably wondering why an award-winning movie star lives in a quaint three-bedroom cottage in Savannah. I imagine he expected some lavish palace bustling with a full staff of servants. Most people do.

"This is the first home my parents bought together." I slip around him and step onto the catwalk that separates the master suite from the two guest rooms.

Halfway across, I stop and rest my forearms on the railing that overlooks the vacant kitchen and hearth room below. Where the hell is Reese? He wouldn't have gone home without checking in with me.

Decker joins me, mimicking my pose, his gaze on the emerald green view beyond the windows.

The open kitchen sits at the back of the house, veneered by a three-story wall of glass that overlooks the pool and the marshy woodland beyond.

"That's the back half of the five-hundred-acre property." I squint against the sunlight spilling through the windows across from us. "There's a forty-acre lake there." I point at the clearing near the tree line. "Two other lakes sit on the north side. Aside from regular maintenance on the running trails, I've kept the land and its wildlife habitats untouched. Do you like to fish?"

"I've never tried. Never been out of the city." He laughs, his mouth hanging open as he stares at me. "Do *you* fish?"

"When I have time. I spent my childhood out there." I nod at the landscape. "Fishing, exploring, chasing rodents, playing in the dirt." They were the best years of my life.

"You have sentimental ties to this place." He studies me for several heartbeats before turning back to the windows. "How do you secure five-hundred acres?"

"An impenetrable fence around the perimeter, a state of the art security system, and the largest team of private security personnel in the business." I peek at his rugged profile. "I don't have a multi-million-dollar mansion, but I spend that much and more on personal protection."

Something moves across his expression. Appreciation? Curiosity? I don't know him well enough to interpret the flickers in his eyes.

"We passed a building just inside the front gate," he says. "Do the guards live there?"

"Some of them. The others rotate on a schedule and sleep there when needed."

"But you don't feel safe."

"Why would you assume—?"

"You carry a gun." He tips his head back and directs his gaze at my lower back.

My heart stutters, and I straighten from my lean against the railing. Apparently, I suck at concealing the tiny handgun beneath my shirt.

"What are you afraid of?" he asks.

You. I swallow the thought. "I saw you talking to my security team on the plane, and Reese told me you had a conversation with Elijah last night. Did you uncover anything juicy?"

"Your head of security wasn't very forthcoming." He casts me a disapproving look. "I'm not interested in gossip, Laynee. Just trying to understand the inner workings of your world and all possible threats to it."

"None of that is your concern. I hire people to protect—"

"Why do you restrain men?"

He's like a hound on a scent, sniffing the air around me, drilling into my eyes, and rummaging through my unspoken answers. Men like him are drawn to women like me. He's attuned to my secrets and senses they're right here, around, against, and within me, clinging to me and calling to him so keenly he can't ignore his instinct to chase. He'll hunt until he obtains what he wants. Until I have nothing left for him to take.

I clench my hands on the railing and give him the response no dominant man wants to hear. "It pleases me to see a man in shackles."

The cords in his forearms flex. "You like the control."

"Yes."

"Makes you feel less vulnerable."

"That's not—"

"You're afraid of me." He holds up a hand, stalling my protest. "Your pretty little neck stiffens every time you look at me. Your breaths are raspy, and you're holding that railing in a death grip."

Fuck. I release the banister and try to relax. It would be easier to be around him if he weren't so brutally gorgeous. The seductive rumble in his voice, the ruthless vibes he puts off, and the fact that he's twelve years younger and stronger are all reminders that he can and will overpower me.

Dressed in ratty jeans and a thin black t-shirt, he exudes a cocky bad-boy edge, one that darkens his flawless beauty. He isn't some vain prissy model like the men I ask for. He's the epitome of a man's man, trained in combat sports and undoubtedly well-versed in pleasuring women.

His dark brown hair looks soft and clean yet somehow stands up in tousled rebellion that make me want to grip and pull. He might've looked younger than twenty-eight if it weren't for his chiseled jawline and day-old stubble. His golden skin glows in the sunlight from the windows, and those sexy hooded eyes, fringed in thick lashes, promise things. Dirty, painful things. I imagine it doesn't take much to bring out the innate animal lurking behind that gaze. I tremble at the thought and hate myself for craving it.

"I know you need time to open up." He leans a hip against the spindles, facing me. "But I'm going to be inflexible, aggressive, and stubborn as hell about eradicating this fear you have of me."

My hands clench. "When are you not those things?"

"When a beautiful woman aims a gun at me." His lips tilt into a half-grin.

"Does that happen often?"

"Only once." His expression turns to stone. "It will never happen again."

My throat seals up.

"Close your eyes." He touches a knuckle beneath my chin.

I open my mouth to object, but his flinty glare steals my voice. He's challenging me to do this, to prove

I'm stronger than my fear.

The logical part of my brain knows he won't cause me bodily harm. That would void the Infidelity agreement, and he needs the income. But there are worse ways to hurt a person. My heart's been kicked, humiliated, and stabbed repeatedly, and I don't trust it around a man like Decker Gabrielli. A man who gets what he wants with a sexy smile and a crook of his finger. He's exactly the kind of man I fall for. And I fall *hard*. So hard it takes years of therapy to get my feet beneath me again.

But I'm stuck with him for a year, and I can't keep my eyes open every second of every day. I need to trust myself. Trust that I won't fall again.

With a steadying breath, I shut my eyes.

His fingers feather across my jaw, joined by his other hand as he cradles my face in the warmth of his touch. All my senses narrow to the shift of his feet, the proximity of his body moving closer, and the palms resting beneath my ears.

Eyes closed, I feel the air stir against my face. My lips part, and my pulse spikes. He's going to kiss me.

Don't freak out. It's just an exchange of breaths. I'm not falling.

Except the instant his breath is replaced by strong lips, my nerve endings flare to life, and my insides burst into flames. His mouth is so warm, so firm and tenacious, gliding sensually, assertively against mine, sparking an electrical chain reaction through my body.

He licks once, twice, and groans, and the deep sound shivers across my skin. His fingers skim into my hair and tighten, holding me gently yet possessively. My knees weaken, and my lungs burn for air.

I gasp as the soft dips of his tongue become

strong thrusts. Coaxing turns into claiming, and when I melt against the hard wall of his chest, the kiss is no longer a kiss. It's a head-to-toe surrender. I'm not just letting it happen. I'm participating, chasing his tongue, pressing closer, deeper, and demanding more.

My grip on the railing tightens, because fuck me, I want to climb his huge frame, tangle my fingers in his hair, and wrench him against me. His breathing quickens, and urgency overrides technique. His tongue feverishly slides against mine, hot and wet and aggressive in a way that demands I keep up, but seductive enough to make me want to.

My God, the man knows how to kiss. Not just with his mouth, but with the rumbling sounds in his chest, the pressure of his fingers in my hair, and the desire fanning through his breaths. He tastes and nibbles and eats at my mouth with passion and commitment. But he doesn't rush, doesn't seem to be racing toward an end goal that involves me naked and pinned beneath him. He kisses me as if all he wants is to savor the taste of my mouth and the friction of our lips. He kisses me as if he could do it all day, a man confidently aware of his skill and its effect on me.

His hand curls around my nape. A massive hand. I try not to pull away, but it's hard. He could snap my neck with a flick of his wrist. Instead, he uses his grip to keep my mouth against his as he turns us to lean his back against the banister.

The position lowers him into a slight recline, making his mouth easier to reach. With my hips in the *V* of his legs, I don't know where to put my hands. But I don't want to break the kiss. I'm too hungry and worked up. My breasts feel heavy, and the throb in my pussy pulses greedily as I suck and lick his tongue while blindly reaching for the railing.

He catches my wrist and guides my palm beneath his shirt. The hot hard surface of his abs startles me. I look down, pulling my mouth from his, to watch my fingers move beneath the black cotton.

The heave of our breaths charge the air between us as I trace steep rows of indentations between bricks of muscle. Firmly holding my neck, he lifts the hem of his shirt, revealing a sculpted torso, smooth skin, and a mouth-watering trail of sparse hair that vanishes beneath the low waist of his jeans. Jeans that strain across his thick swollen length.

Heat spreads between my legs and soaks my panties. My fingers shake, and my pulse thrums. I ache to lick every ridge, sink my teeth into his flesh, and suck all his hard edges.

Holy shit, what has he done to me? His kiss turned me into a panting hot mess, and now I'm drooling over his sexy-as-fuck body. I bet the bastard's gloating.

I peer up at him through my lashes, but instead of a cocky smirk, I find his lips swollen and parted, eyes molten, and expression dazed.

"Fuck, Laynee." He blinks. "Give me your mouth."

His words... That raw look...

My brain short circuits, and I launch at him, fusing our lips and roaming my hands. Every muscled hill and valley is a playground for my fingers. There isn't a squishy spot on his body, not a single ounce of fat. It's not fair. I work my ass off in the gym and still have bits that jiggle and droop.

He chuckles against my mouth and grabs my wrists. "What's with the claws?"

Oh. Oops. I glance at my trimmed fingernails and relax my hands. "I'm cursing the injustice in…" Sliding my palms up his defined chest, I lift the shirt to expose tight, dark nipples and chiseled pecs. "All of this."

He glances down at his perfect body, his brows knitting together. "Injustice? I work hard—"

"While you're living with me, you will not slack on your workouts."

He laughs. "Is that an order?"

"Yes." I bite down on my smile. "I have an extensive home gym. If you need weights or equipment added, let Reese know."

"I don't take orders, Laynee, but I'll make a deal with you." He guides my fingers across his washboard abs. "Touch me like this every day, and I'll keep myself fit."

"Deal." Now I have a legitimate reason to grope him, one that has nothing to do with my self-destructive addiction to dominant men.

Leaning against the banister, he rests his hands on his spread thighs and watches me caress the warm marbled terrace of his torso. I don't stare at the erection straining his jeans, but I'm painfully aware of its presence.

This man is a paradox. The feral fire burning in his eyes says he wants to explore my body the way I'm exploring his. He could tackle me to the floor this very instant, use his strength and size to force my legs open, and take what he wants. Yet he hasn't touched me below the neck.

"We need to talk about rules." With great effort, I pull my hands away and step back.

"Yes. Tell me about the rules you're going to set, and I'll tell you how I'm going to ignore them."

"Decker—"

"Or we can make more deals. That approach seems to work with you."

"What do you mean?" My hackles bristle.

"I give an inch. You give an inch. Let's start with our sleeping arrangements." He bends down and grabs his duffel bag. "Which room is yours?"

I'm still burning up from that kiss, and he wants to discuss sharing a bed? I shake my head, arms crossing defensively.

"You're going to give on this." He towers over me, the force of his gaze punctuating the command in his voice. "Tell me what I need to give in return."

He's smart, manipulative, and arrestingly handsome—a menacing combination for a man who kisses with unholy passion. He arouses me as much as he scares the crap out of me. I need to put space between us before I let him stomp all over my life.

"All right." I raise my chin and meet his eyes. "You can sleep in my room—"

"In your bed."

"Fine. In my bed, *sleeping* only, if you comply with my demand."

His eyebrows pull together.

"You and Reese." My voice grows husky just thinking about it. "I want to watch him suck your cock."

"No." His shoulders snap back. "Something else."

"That's the deal. Take it or leave it."

"My answer isn't going to change." He grinds his teeth.

"Then your room is this way." I pivot and head toward the guest rooms at the end of the catwalk.

"He's your buffer." His voice whispers with realization, stopping my feet. "You use him as a barrier between you and whatever this thing is that scares you."

A swallow lodges in my throat, and I force myself to turn around and face him. "Seeing two men together turns me on, Decker. That's all it is."

"No, this goes beyond a simple kink." He rubs a hand across his stubble, studying me. "You're afraid of intimacy. Maybe not sex, but the deeper feelings, like trust, dependency... *Love.* Tell me why. What happened?"

His gaze is too perceptive, absorbing every tic in my expression as I gulp down my weaknesses and try to look tough. But I'm not tough, and if I give him a bullshit answer, he'll see right through it.

"I've known you less than a day." I plead with my eyes. *Stop pushing so hard.* "You're demanding trust that you haven't earned."

He pulls in a breath and releases it. "You're right."

That's it? His easy acceptance leaves me stuttering.

With his duffel bag in hand, he turns away and strides back toward the stairway. *Not* in the direction of the guest rooms.

"Where are you going?" I hurry after him. "Your room's the other way."

He veers toward the alcove off the landing.

My pulse leaps to my throat. "You can't go in there."

Reaching the only door on this end of the upper floor, he barges into my bedroom. After a quick scan of the large suite, he drops his bag, kicks off his Converse, and stretches out on the king-size mattress. "Why does a tiny woman need such a big bed?"

The pound of my heart roars in my ears. This is my safe space, my sanctuary. Other than Reese, I've never let a man in my room. "I'm not comfortable with you being in here, Decker."

"I know you're not," he says gently and pats the space beside him. "Come here."

The wood floorboards turn into quicksand.

"Look." He laces his fingers behind his head. "My hands will stay here."

Our eyes lock, and I know I should tell him to go play his games on some other gullible woman. But the thought of him looking at someone else the way he looks at me makes my fingernails dig into my palms.

The petrified excitement he instills in me makes my thighs wet. The deep confidence in his timbre tempts me to beg to be used and owned. His mere presence urges me to rush toward the same snare that has caught me again and again. Even as I know it's a trap, one that will eventually hurt me, I gravitate toward it. Toward him.

Sliding off my heels, I wipe my palms on my jeans. My breathing quickens as I cross the room and lie on my back beside him, with a foot of space between us.

"Did you decorate the room yourself?" He glances around the suite.

"*That's* what you want to talk about?"

"If it sheds light on the woman I'm living with."

Fair enough. "I do my own decorating, if you can call it that. When I moved back here two years ago, I added the French doors and the screened room and had the bathroom and closet enlarged and modernized."

Other than that, it's rather unexceptional for celebrity standards. The furniture is mismatched. Classic pieces leftover from my parents intermix with contemporary armchairs and modern art. The variety of color and style is haphazard. Lots of soft fabrics and vivid shades of turquoise and yellow. I wanted warmth and comfort and didn't give much thought to design.

"Tell me about your schedule." Reclined on his back, he angles his neck to look at me.

"When I'm not traveling or on a movie set?"

He nods.

"Well..." I roll to my side and lean up on an elbow, facing him. "I work out two hours every morning. My days are dedicated to whatever I'm involved in at the time, whether it's reading scripts, practicing lines, interviewing, or dealing with my agent, publicist, or whoever is nagging me for something."

"Are your evenings open?"

"Generally."

"I have a counteroffer on our sleeping arrangements." He licks his lips. "Share your bed with me, and in exchange, I'll teach you self-defense."

"I can hire a professional instructor if I want—"

"I was one of the best combat sports instructors in the business." His jaw flexes. "I can teach you how to overpower men bigger and stronger than me, and that skill will go a long way in annihilating your fears." He hardens his eyes. "I'm going to sleep beside you, Laynee, but I want you to want me here. Training with you every day will give me an opportunity to earn your trust."

What woman wouldn't want him in her bed? Hell, what woman wouldn't want to get sweaty with him on wrestling mats? I let myself imagine him in nothing but thin shorts hanging low on his hips, his muscles bunching and straining as he twists that magnificent physique through grappling techniques.

My core spasms hard and deep. “Will you be shirtless during these training sessions?”

He winks at me with a cocky nod of his head. “You betcha.”

CHAPTER 11

Decker

I spend the next month settling into a surreal reality, one that centers all my focus on a single woman, tests the limits of my patience, and compels me to search for random distractions. Like baking a peach pie.

Leaning over the kitchen island, I poke at the flaky crust. Juice bubbles through the slits in the top, fuming the air with the syrupy aroma of awesomeness. It looks pretty badass for a guy who used to live on instant noodles and frozen meals.

"It's ready." I grab a pie cutter.

"I can't eat that, Decker." Laynee stands on the other side of the island, dead-eying the pie with murderous longing.

"You can, and you will." I cut a huge slice and set it on the plate in front of her.

"Is it sugar-free, gluten-free, fat-free, and guilt-free?" She nudges the dish away.

"Fuck no. It's pie, not toilet paper." I push it back toward her.

"I'll take her piece…and mine." Reese glances up from his laptop at the kitchen table and grins.

"I made this for *you*." I give her the look, the one that quickens her breaths and flushes her cheeks.

"Don't do that." She points at my face. "Those sleepy eyes might work on Reese, but I'm immune."

"I don't give Reese any kind of goddamn look," I growl. "And just because you're stubborn as hell, doesn't mean I don't affect you. Admit it."

She drops her gaze and pinches her cupid lips between her teeth.

"I make your heart race." I lean in.

"Decker..."

"I make your thighs tremble." Heat pulses along the length of my shaft.

She inhales sharply.

"Is your pussy wet?" I whisper.

Her eyes flutter closed. Behind her, Reese ducks his head and focuses on the laptop.

"I want to fuck you." I lift her chin with the tip of my finger. "And you want that so badly it consumes you."

She opens her eyes. "I offered you a deal, and you turned it down."

I yank my hand back and shove it through my hair.

We've made three deals since I moved in.

One, I keep myself fit by working out with her every morning in exchange for her frequent and agonizing caresses. *Caresses she refuses to extend below my belt.*

Two, I teach her self-defense in the evenings, and she lets me sleep beside her every night. *With a foot of* don't-touch-me *space between us.*

Three, I prepare her food, and she eats all her meals with me. *If I follow her ridiculous dietary restrictions.*

The woman has more money than God, yet she doesn't employ housekeepers, butlers, chefs, or anyone outside of Reese and her security personnel. Locked in her office all day with a phone at her ear and her nose buried in contracts and screenplays, she needs a full staff. But she doesn't trust people in her home. I admire her prudence and tenacity, but watching her scramble to throw meals together or skip them completely pisses me off. So I took over the cooking.

Reese runs her errands, does her shopping, and manages her schedule. While he's available to her around the clock, he usually only comes by during the day and spends his evenings doing hell knows what at his loft in downtown Savannah.

Her lack of live-in employees is both a blessing and a torture. Other than Reese's daily visits, I'm alone with her most of the time.

And all I think about is sex.

Every morning, I run with her on the trails and imagine tossing her to the ground and fucking her beautiful mouth. Every evening, I roll around with her on the gym floor, training her how to fight comfortably on her back while thinking about pounding my cock deep inside her.

Bedtime is the worst. When I lie beside her, I curse the deal she won't back down from, the one where she'll have sex with me, if I let Reese suck my cock.

My hands fist. She knows I want her. I tell her as often as she sees the evidence in my pants. But she has this regal, untouchable air about her. She sleeps in head-to-toe silk, wears body-covering workout gear like a shield, and locks the door when she showers and changes clothes. I share a room with the woman and haven't seen so much as her naked stomach.

To think I was worried about how I would get it up for some repulsive cunt in a strap-on. Instead, I'm endlessly horny, celibate, and lured to utter torment by

Laynee's seductive kisses. She might button herself up like a nun, but she licks my mouth like a greedy, slutty sex-kitten. I steal those hot kisses countless times a day, but when it gets too heated or my hands grow too bold, she pushes me away. Every. Fucking. Time.

She's stuck on this concept that Reese is a fail-safe, as if his participation in her sex life protects her physically and emotionally. I know I scare her, and her bullshit offer is her way of unmanning me. What's more emasculating than ordering a straight man to submit to another man's mouth?

Someone hurt her. I just don't know who, when, or how badly. Every time I breach the conversation, she refuses to talk.

Just like she refuses to eat the damn pie.

I grab a fork and shovel a bite into my mouth. Flavor explodes on my tongue, the taste of summertime and temptation, just like her lips.

"It's warm and wet and sinful." I pin her with a simmering look. "Reminds me of something else, though I can't be sure, because I'm in the longest dry spell of my life."

"Oh?" She narrows her eyes. "How long?"

"What?"

"Your dry spell. How long has it been?"

"Four fucking weeks."

Her face reddens. "Y—You've been *here* for four weeks. Did you have sex with someone the night you met me?"

"No." I think it was the night before I was fired from Blue Dixie. "There's been no one since you." I seem to have forgotten every woman prior to Laynee Somerset.

"You poor thing. You must really be suffering."

She grimaces with half of her mouth, and that down-turned corner tilts away from me, as if she's trying to hide her jealous reaction.

I scoop another bite and hold it toward her lips. "Open."

"No." She faces me head-on and flattens her palms on the counter.

"Now."

"I said no."

"But you mean yes." I harden my tone.

"I saw someone wearing a t-shirt the other day that said, *No means the gag isn't tight enough.*"

What the fuck? Has she been gagged? Forced against her will? A wave of rage crashes through me. Her expression is blank, a little tight around her eyes. It tells me nothing.

I hold the fork in front of her, refusing to back down but at the same time needing her to understand. "I'm not that guy."

"Oh, so this whole *do-what-I-say,* harass, and intimidate thing you're doing is…*what?* An unfortunate mistake?" A playful gleam flashes in her eyes.

She's fucking with me?

"Just put the pie in your pie hole and shut up." I shove the drippy bite against her lips.

Her mouth pops open and in goes the fork. Making her eat this is about me taking some damn control over this relationship. But as I slide the tines free and devour every twitch in her face while she chews, I find that her reaction means more to me than my victory. I want her to enjoy the treat simply because I want her to be happy.

She closes her eyes, swallows, and moans with her fingers against her mouth. The sound reverberates along my cock.

"Jesus, Decker." Her gaze locks with mine. "That's unbelievable. Were you lying when you said you never cooked in New York?"

"No." I lift another bite toward her tantalizing mouth. "It's no wonder why I never get this reaction from the tasteless shit you demand I make." I touch the forkful of pie against her lips. "You can bet your sweet ass there'll be more where this came from." *Just to see that blissful look on her face.*

"I have an audition next month for a lead role." She leans back and stares at the hovering fork. "I really can't eat…another… Okay, maybe just one more bite."

Her sexy doll-like lips wrap around the tines and slide off the morsel. Another sinful expression of pleasure, more moans, and now I know the true meaning of hell. She's killing me slowly and mercilessly.

I go back for another scoop and pretend my swollen cock isn't painfully throbbing against my zipper.

She holds her hand out, shaking her head. "I need to…" She darts to the fridge and rummages inside. "I need something filling and healthy or I'll eat the whole pie. Where are my protein drinks?"

I could tell her I shoved them to the back, but I'm not saying shit while she's bent over like that, with her fuckable ass filling my vision. Encased in denim, her cheeks are perfectly round and firm and molded in the exact size of my hands. Her waistband slides low, exposing a sliver of skin, Venusian dimples on either side of her tailbone, and…

What the hell is that?

Edging closer, I bend down, zeroing in on a faint

white welt of twisted flesh. An inch in length, the scar is jagged and wide. Not something sustained on an operating table, but rather from sharp force trauma.

I reach for the hem of her shirt. "What happened—?"

Her head flies up, catches the glass shelving, and scatters condiments and produce. The collision sends her falling back on her butt. I grab her arm to catch her, but she jerks away, dropping a protein bottle and shoving down the back of her shirt.

"Shit, you startled me." She climbs to her feet, tugging on that damn shirt.

"Turn around." I make an impatient swirling gesture with my finger. "Show me your back."

"Excuse me?" Her neck stiffens, and her eyes blink rapidly.

"You heard me." My voice is low and sharp, brooking no argument. "While you're lifting your shirt, you can tell me how you got the scar."

CHAPTER 12

Decker

Once again, I'm demanding answers, but this time, Laynee's going to give me something. I don't care if it takes all night. I'm finished with her secrets.

"I don't have to tell you shit." Her eyes spark with equal parts fury and fear.

"Laynee," I say in a softer tone. "I'm not the enemy. I won't hurt you."

A chiming ringtone blares from the counter behind her.

She whirls toward the phone and connects the call. "Violet?"

My pulse hammers in my ears as I fight to keep my agitation in check. I suspect her publicist is calling about Laynee's trip to L.A. tomorrow. The trip I'm going on whether they like it or not.

"I haven't been ignoring you. No, that's—" She sighs into the phone. "Fine. I'm listening." She casts me a glare and marches out of the kitchen.

Fuck this. I've been nice. I've been patient. I've followed her exhausting rules and given her miles of time and space. It's not working.

I turn toward Reese, who's watching me with a guarded expression.

"Tell me that's not a knife wound on her back." I point at the doorway she disappeared through.

"You've only been here a month, man." He sits back and crosses his arms. "You need to be patient."

Not answering my question is an answer in itself.

"She doesn't respond to patience." I charge toward him, bracing a hand on the back of his chair and the other on the table in front of him. "Who hurt her?"

His lips press into a line, and he averts his gaze.

If Laynee Somerset was attacked or hospitalized, it would've been in the news. When I arrived in Savannah, I spent the first couple days scouring the Internet and acquainting myself with everything the media says about her. I learned that her ex, Blake Harridan, allegedly cheated on her, but she refuses to confirm the speculation publicly—or privately with me. She's the most clammed up person I've ever met, and it's driving me to madness.

How does a superstar, one who's photographed as much as Laynee, hide a suspicious scar from the press? I have a thousand other questions, but I'm starting with that one.

Stepping away from Reese, I snatch his laptop off the table and carry it to the island. When I glance down at the screen, my ass clenches.

"Chics with dicks?" I stare with dumb shock at the website of leather-clad women with huge plastic cocks.

"That's not..." His chair screeches on the wood floor behind me. "It's a harness with—"

"I don't care." I open a new tab in the browser and search on images of Laynee.

"What are you doing?" His footsteps approach.

"Looking for answers."

"You won't find them on-line."

He stands behind me and shoulder-surfs while I

flip through hundreds of red-carpet photos taken of her over the past twenty years. Almost every gown she wore in her twenties was open-back. I zoom in on the images and find unmarred skin instead of a scar. One in particular, snapped at the Oscars six years ago, shows the full-length of her spine, damn near exposing her ass crack. Increasing the magnification, I study the high-resolution image. No scar.

"You need to stop this," Reese says behind me.

"If you're not going to be helpful, go the fuck away." I point at the doorway without removing my eyes from the screen.

Something happened to her in the last six years. Narrowing my search, I look through galleries of photos taken during that time frame. Every image confirms that six years ago she stopped wearing backless gowns or any kind of revealing clothing. There are no bikini-on-the-beach pictures, nothing that exposes any part of her back. And she already admitted she uses body doubles to do the nude scenes in her movies.

Dread curls in my stomach.

"What happened six years ago?" I turn toward Reese and give him the full brunt of my glare.

He drags a hand down his face and spins toward the sound of heels clicking through the doorway.

Laynee steps into the kitchen, clutching the phone to her abdomen, gaze locked on the laptop. "What are you looking at?"

"How were you injured six years ago?" My voice is abrasive, but it can't be helped. I've reached my limit.

She moves to the sink and fills a glass with water, draining half of it in one gulp.

I shake with the urge to bend her over my knee and spank her until she screams her secrets. But her stiff-as-a-board posture tells me that would be a terrible mistake.

"Talk to me, Laynee." I close the laptop and shove it aside. "I'm assuming the worst here."

She grips the edge of the counter and stares blankly out the window over the sink. The empty silence continues long enough to confirm she's not going to answer.

"I'm just gonna…" Reese inches toward the doorway. "I'll go get you some more holes for your jeans."

I glance down at the ripped-up denim on my legs. I came to Savannah with the threads on my back and a change of clothes in my bag. Now I have a wardrobe worth more than my annual income from Infidelity, thanks to Reese's enthusiasm in shopping on Laynee's dime. I wear the shit he hangs in my closet. He has excellent taste, though I'll never admit that to him. But sometimes I put on my old jeans, like today, just to annoy him.

"Sit down." I direct him to the chair beside the kitchen table and pace through the room. "Here's what we're going to do. I'll tell you what I've pieced together, and you'll fill in the blanks and correct my assumptions."

If Laynee doesn't talk, maybe Reese will.

He lowers into the chair, and she faces me, hugging her arms around her waist.

I approach her slowly. "In the past two years, you've only had sex with two men." My chest constricts with irrational jealousy. "I assume neither of those men saw you naked." *Given the way she conceals that scar.*

She stares at the floor and gives a weak nod, reinforcing my suspicion that it's not just me she hides her body from. She wears clothing like armor, the same way she uses Reese as a barrier against intimacy.

"Why those two men?" I ask. "What did they do to earn your trust?"

"First off, they never had my trust." Her arms tighten around her mid-section. "They accepted my deal, so I gave them an hour inside my body. It's as simple as that."

Her words make me feel so insanely, barbarously possessive of her. I've never experienced that primal reaction with anyone, and I haven't even fucked her. But that isn't the real issue. She's discussing sex with verbiage like *deal* and *gave them an hour*.

I've kissed this woman. She's brimming with passion and raw sexuality. When I eventually enter her body, I have no doubt she'll scream and writhe and unravel around me, and it'll last a helluva lot longer than an hour.

"Explain the deal they accepted." I bend my knees, trying to catch her lowered gaze.

"They let Reese suck them and fuck them while I watched."

Exactly what I expected. They surrendered to her on a psychological level, submitted to Reese physically, and therefore proved themselves safe enough for her to have sex with. *While she kept her clothes on.*

The image of her with other men makes me want to punch something, but I breathe through it and focus. Something doesn't add up. "Reese fucked them? Not the other way around?"

"Yes," she mutters to the floor.

I glance at him, noting the tension in his shoulders. "Reese is a bottom."

Her head shoots up, eyes on the other man. "No,

he isn't."

"That's weird. I've only known him a month, yet I know he doesn't like to do the fucking. You've known him for how long?"

"Don't do this." Reese's expression tightens.

"Laynee." I grip the counter on either side of her hips. "How long have you known Reese?"

"Ten years." She looks at Reese accusingly. "Why does he think you're a bottom?"

"It's not..." He picks at something on his jeans. "It's nothing."

"Reese?" She straightens, staring at him with bright damp eyes.

"We're good." He tips his head back and sighs. "Let's just drop it."

"No, we're not good." She pushes my arm away and moves toward the island, bracing her hands on the surface. "Why didn't you tell me?"

"I was trying to help." He shrugs.

He's an enabler. *Was.* I'm taking control of her fears going forward, and we're fixing this my way.

"You two can work out your communication issues later." I lean against the counter beside her and hook my thumbs in my back pockets. "Before those two men, you were with Blake Harridan. You married four years ago. Divorced two years later. Because he cheated on you."

"Congratulations." Acid laces her voice. "You know how to Google."

I've never wanted to bring unholy hell upon a person I've never met, but I'm burning to do exactly that now. "I'll kill him."

"Please, don't." She rubs her head as wariness leaks into her expression. "My involvement with him has done enough damage to my reputation."

"He was a nobody when Laynee met him." Reese folds his arms on the table, his voice clipped with disgust. "Just an extra in one of her movies. She propelled his career and made him who he is today."

And the bastard thanked her by cheating on her. I don't know if it's the scar on her back or her fear of men, but I have a godawful feeling that adultery wasn't his only crime.

I step into her space and lower to her height. "When did you meet him?"

"A month before we married." Her face crumples. "I've made some really poor choices when it comes to men."

If she's only known Blake for four years, he's not responsible for the scar. And she just said *men*. Multiple poor choices.

"Who were you with before Blake?" I ask.

Pale lines bracket her mouth before a stubborn mask slides down, shielding her emotions. "How about we put *you* on the spot? Who have you been fucking for the past twenty-eight years, Decker Gabrielli?"

I consider her question for a moment. She already knows my secrets, so I have nothing to hide. "I didn't have sex thirteen of those twenty-eight years."

Confusion etches her face before her blue eyes pop wide. "You lost your virginity at thirteen?"

"Grew up in a rough neighborhood. Single mother. Poor supervision."

She nods as if she understands, but she doesn't. How could she? She and I come from two very different worlds.

"According to your profile," she says, "you've never been in a committed relationship. Does that mean you've never been in love?"

"Not even close." I rub the back of my neck. "I rarely sleep with the same woman twice."

"Why?"

If I tell her I avoid relationships because committed women are needy and boring, it'll give her one more reason to keep me at arm's length. Instead, I dig deep and give her a truthful, more vulnerable answer. "I'm searching for the one I want to chase forever. The one I can't walk away from."

Her lips part. Her eyes shine, and her perky tits rise and fall with her breaths—all of it fills me with immense pleasure. I could spend the rest of my life watching her react that way. *While she's bouncing on my cock.*

"I need to go." Reese rises from the chair. "I'll be late for a date."

"Chic with a plastic dick?" I ask.

"One can hope." He walks around the island, grabs his laptop, and kisses Laynee on the cheek. "See you tomorrow."

She watches him leave and shakes her head. "I should've known. I mean, I know he likes to be ordered around. It turns him on. But I didn't associate that with…positioning and…sexual partners." She scrapes a hand through her hair. "God, I can be so oblivious sometimes."

"I know a thing or two about being oblivious."

"You?" She laughs bitterly. "Nothing gets past you."

I pace through the kitchen and debate the wisdom in correcting her. It would mean baring my insecurities. Maybe that's what we both need. A little humble pie would do me good, and it might help her perceive me as something other than a threatening shadow looming over her.

Lowering onto the stool at the island, I leave enough room between my spread legs and the counter for her to stand.

"Come here." At her hesitation, I soften my tone. "Please."

She steps into the *V* of my legs and leans her butt against the counter, arms crossed over her chest.

"I had this one student at my school." I place a hand on the edge beside her hip and rest my thumb on the waistband of her jeans. "A nine-year-old boy with a wicked-sharp sense of humor and this huge infectious smile. God, the kid was always smiling." I swallow past a tight throat. "Then one day, he stopped smiling."

I inch my thumb upward until I make contact with the soft skin of her waist.

She doesn't yank my hand away, and instead slides her fingers across my shoulders. "Go on."

"His mom lost her job. Single-parent family. Money was already tight. The kid had so much passion in the sport, and I loved teaching him." I smile in memory. "He reminded me a lot of myself. When his mom couldn't pay for his lessons, I took him on pro bono." Old pain flares in my chest. "The boy's smile never returned. I thought it was related to problems at home."

"Decker," she whispers, guiding my forehead to rest against her flat stomach. "You don't have to tell me."

"I need you to understand." Gripping her hips, I lean back to see her face. "That boy spent all his free time at my gym. It was his escape from the harsh reality of his shit life. I was his teacher, his mentor, his *protector*. I looked him in the eye every fucking day, and I didn't see what was happening to him. What was happening in my own fucking gym." Emotion roars through my veins and thickens my voice. "Do you know why he stopped smiling, Laynee?"

"Yes. I know." She caresses my face. "It wasn't your fault."

"I didn't do those…unspeakable things, but I didn't prevent it, either."

"You stopped it, Decker. I read the reports Infidelity sent over. One of those boys trusted you enough to tell you. I know you're the one who turned in Adam Lamont and funded the lawyers for those kids."

My stomach cramps with remembered horror. I've never felt more like a failure than I did the day I learned what was happening. "I can't do that again, Laynee. I can't look at you and be with you and not know what's happening to you." I press a hand against her lower back, directly over the scar. "Tell me who hurt you."

She stiffens. "It's in the past."

"It's not." Anger rises through my tone. "It's right fucking here. A living, breathing thing wedged between us. I want it gone."

"I've worked so hard to do exactly that." Her voice cracks, and she pulls in a ragged breath. "It's cost me time and job opportunities and money…so much fucking money to keep it out of the media and make it disappear."

"Is that why you refuse to tell me? You think I'll sell the story?" I grind my teeth. "You don't trust me."

Her hands slide through my hair, and her eyes travel over my face. "I trust you, and that's the problem. Apart from Reese, every single person I've trusted has hurt me." She smiles sadly. "You'd have better luck with me if I didn't trust you."

Jesus, fuck. What am I supposed to do with that? "You trusted the person who gave you that scar?"

She lowers her arms and slips from my grasp. Tugging down the back of her shirt, she exits the kitchen, as if the conversation is over.

I stalk after her, determination steeling my spine. I could rip off that shirt and sweep her to the floor in two seconds flat. An armlock would have her squealing answers to my questions in the two seconds that follow. She's learned a few self-defense maneuvers over the past couple weeks, but she's nowhere near my skill level. Physically overpowering her would certainly choke any trust she has in me.

But that's not what I want. She needs some control in her life. I can give her all the control she wants within the limits I set for her, and one of those limits is the goddamn wall she's erected around herself. I'm going to break through it, starting tonight.

CHAPTER 13

Decker

My usual approach with women could be simplified with words such as chase and catch, hard and fast, in and out. But as I follow Laynee up the stairs and into the bedroom, the urge to grab her hair and drag her to the bed is overshadowed by the reason I'm chasing her.

For the first time in my life, I'm going to beguile a woman into removing her clothes to help her, rather than help myself. Though I'm not a fucking saint. I will most certainly enjoy the view.

"You have two options." I prowl behind her, eying her luscious ass.

She stops in the center of the bedroom but doesn't turn around.

"Option one. Keep your shirt on and tell me about the scar." I pace a circle around her, my posture relaxed and casual. "Option two. Remove the shirt and keep your secrets tonight."

Her eyes leap to mine, and I can't read anything in her expression beyond the deer-in-headlights look.

"If you choose to go to bed without explaining the scar…" I ghost my fingertips along her jawline. "You'll sleep without a shirt. Every night. In my arms."

She turns her head away from my touch. "I get that what happened with those kids made you overly concerned and paranoid. I'm sorry for that. I really am."

With a deep breath, she steps back. "But you can take your controlling, high-handed ultimatums and shove them up your ass." She stands taller, eyes blazing. "Let me remind you that you accepted this job for money. You're getting paid to look pretty on my arm and keep your mouth shut. That does not include prying into my business. Whatever your incentive is—"

"You." I shove my face in hers. "Your smile. Your body. Rigorous, mutually-pleasurable, savage sex. *You* are my incentive." I prowl around her, gliding a knuckle along the curves of her shoulders and raising goosebumps on her arms. "I think Infidelity knew exactly what they were doing when they paired us together. You don't need a submissive man who will conform to your orders and enable your misery. You need a man who will erase your insecurities, protect you from the shit that haunts you, and fight for and with you every time you push him away."

Her chest heaves. Her chin juts out, and her fingers curl at her sides.

"You want to treat me like a hired escort?" I stop in front of her and hold my hands loosely behind my back. "Remove your clothes and get your ass on the bed. I'll make you come for hours with my fingers, my mouth, and my cock. You won't even have to talk to me. You'll get what you paid for, and I'll get my money. Because that's all I am to you."

Her nostrils flare, and her eyes turn to slits.

"You don't like that?" Frustration vibrates through my voice. "Too fucking bad. Unlike the last two men you let into your body, I'm not going anywhere. When I fuck you, you'll beg me to stay. You'll beg every fucking night. If all I am is a whore for you to prance around in front of the cameras, I'm going to be a whore in every sense of the word."

"You're not a whore." A sheen of wetness glazes her eyes. "You don't understand how difficult this is for me."

"Then help me understand."

She stares at my chest, and her entire body begins to shake. I'm tempted to back down, because goddammit, I want to shelter and comfort her, not tear her apart. But she needs to push past this paralyzing apprehension, an effort that may unleash some painful emotions. I can't protect her from that, but I'll help her through it.

I gave her a choice. She'll either tell me about the scar tonight, or she'll show it to me. I've already seen it, so I'm not surprised when she reaches for the hem of her shirt and lifts it upward.

It's an agonizingly slow reveal. Her arms tremble, and her breathing quickens with each inch of bared skin. I ache to remove her hands and complete the task for her. But this is her milestone, a significant one if she hasn't shown her body to another man in two years.

When the shirt clears her head and drops to the floor, I'm gifted with an arresting view of creamy flawless skin and full globes of flesh overflowing from a pink lace bra. Her tiny waist curves in like an hourglass, the jeans low and snug on her narrow hips.

Expressionless, she gathers her hair over one shoulder and twists it into a golden rope down her chest.

"You're exquisite," I say in a guttural voice.

Her face falls. She closes her eyes, covers her quivering lips, and shakes her head. I don't understand her reaction until she pivots and gives me her back.

A shocked sound claws up my throat, and I snap

my mouth shut before it escapes. I don't see the scar near her tailbone, not amid the war zone of welted flesh.

I can't even begin to count how many puckered white marks riddle her shoulder blades and both sides of her spine. Her back is a soul-gutting battlefield of brutality, and low on her waist is the outlier, the scar I spotted in the kitchen. It's separated from the rest as if whatever marred her back swung wide and wildly off to the side.

I have to remind myself to breathe. My vision blurs, and my head pounds with questions. Her injuries were neither accidental nor methodical. Someone punctured her over and over, viciously, intently, with a rancor and vehemence of passion.

My hands shake violently, and my gut coils with anguish. I need to say something, but I'm at a loss for words. She won't want my pity, and by removing her shirt, she chose the option that frees her from answering my questions.

Then I'm hit with dumb realization. Someone attacked her back, and here I am, towering over her, *behind her*, more than twice her size, needlessly putting her in a vulnerable position.

With deep, even breaths, I slowly lower to my knees. A tremor skates up her spine. She wraps her arms around her torso and stands still. I hate the silence between us, but I keep my mouth shut, afraid I'll spook her.

On my knees and eye-level with the lower points of her shoulder blades, I'm in arm's reach of every part of her body. I start at her feet, lightly curling my fingers around her ankles.

She shifts slightly and tips her head forward,

watching my hands. I glide them up the fronts of her legs, feathering my fingers over the denim as I touch my forehead to her back. She pulls in a ragged breath, holds it, and releases it with a gentle sigh.

An exhilarating rush of warmth fills my chest. She's not running away, not shoving at my hands. This is the most I've ever touched her, and I don't want to stop.

When my caresses reach the bare skin above her waistband, she shivers. I keep going, leaning back to skim my palms across her back. Some of the scars bump against my fingers, but most are smooth and soft to the touch. Her chest heaves faster, harder, as I stroke each wound. I'm so fucking proud of her for not jerking away.

I'm also insanely and inappropriately aroused. I can't help it. She feels so damn warm and feminine and small in my hands. The impulse to trap her in my arms and fuck her to orgasm heats my muscles and fires my pulse. I want this woman at a primitive, carnal level, but I'm overcome with another stronger sensation, an emotion that goes so much deeper than sex. Possessiveness? Loyalty? Admiration? I feel all those things and more.

My fingers bump against the bra strap. I raise my head to watch the tension in her shoulders as I undo the hooks.

She doesn't jerk when I slide the straps off her arms. Doesn't flinch when I rub my hands up and down her back. Doesn't so much as breathe when I caress each and every scar, trying and failing to count them all. There's at least fifteen…twenty… I give up as my blood pressure rises with the need to avenge every strike that impaled her beautiful body.

Sliding my knees against the backs of her feet, I press against her tiny frame and wrap my hands around her hips. She's so small my fingers meet at her navel. I could crush her without effort, and I know she knows this, which makes her cooperation profoundly significant.

"Thank you." I touch my lips to her spine. "For giving this to me. I can't imagine what it's cost you, but it's a gift I won't take for granted."

"Twenty-six." She grips my fingers, holding them against the hollow of her belly. "Twenty-six stab wounds."

My throat closes up, and my heart slams against my ribs.

Someone stabbed her twenty-six times. Someone she trusted. Is the motherfucker running free? In prison? Dead?

Red clouds my vision, and adrenaline swamps through my veins.

"No questions," she whispers. "Not tonight."

"Right." I swallow, breathe, and curse my stupidity in giving her that option. "No questions."

"But you'll hold me?" Hope threads through her voice. "I can sleep in your arms?"

Everything inside me reacts. The bones in my fingers, the blood beneath my skin, the air in my lungs, the beat of my heart—all of it stretches, lifts, and reaches for her.

Her walls might not have fallen, but they're bending. *She's* bending. Everything has changed.

I hook my arms around her hips and breathe against her back, "I want that more than anything."

CHAPTER 14

Laynee

My heart hurtles on a loop of *whatamIdoing-whatamIdoing-whatamIdoing?* I force down the panic, because deep down, I know Decker's intent is to help me, not hurt me.

But his concern is what scares me the most. He's gorgeous and commanding and confident. Add magnanimous into the mix and I don't trust myself around him. I have an addiction, and he's my poison. Once I sample him, I'll keep going back until my need becomes compulsive and interferes with my life, my job, and my well-being.

But he's not going to let my protests against sex slide much longer. He can have any woman he wants, and apparently, he doesn't go without. Not if a month is his longest dry spell.

I hate the possessive ferocity that bubbles inside me when I think about him with other women. It's on the tip of my tongue to remind him he signed an agreement that made him mine for a year. But that would sound desperate and crazy. Because it is. Especially when I won't let him fuck me.

I want him to fuck me. I want it so badly I think of nothing else. It's been too long, and to say I enjoy sex is an understatement. I crave it. *Too much.* Watching Reese with other men gives me vicarious pleasure, but it's not the same as being held in strong arms, trembling beneath adoring lips, and fusing with another body, heart, and soul.

And this is the problem. I can't fuck without pouring my emotions into it. When I'm with a man, he's my everything. His opinions, his desires, his every wish means the world to me. I want to please him and make him happy. But it's too much power to give a person. I learned that the hard, painful way.

Reese was the solution for this, and it worked fine with the last two men I had sex with. They were submissive and nonthreatening. Reese never left the room, and I kept my clothes on. The temptation to make it more than a physical act didn't materialize. I intended to treat whoever Infidelity paired me with the same way.

But they sent me Decker Gabrielli.

Kneeling behind me, he uses his grip on my waist to turn me to face him. I'm tempted to cover myself, but he saw my scars. Showing him my bare chest pales in comparison.

Or so I thought.

He lifts his eyes, and his hands tighten on my hips. His pupils dilate, and a slow smile builds on his beautiful mouth. He's so much taller than me that even on his knees, his face is right there, level with my boobs, his breath warm and tantalizing against my skin.

My nipples harden, and he growls low and deep, like an animal. A hungry, sexy, top-of-the-food-chain animal. He might be on his knees, but he's the one in control, orchestrating every move, and making me wait for whatever comes next. Hell, he manipulates the speed of my pulse, the throb between my legs, and every damn breath I take.

I'm in trouble. I recognize all the warning signs—the flutter in my belly, the wetness between my legs, the overwhelming need to curl up in his arms—yet I can't stop the words from shooting past my lips. "If I'm sleeping without a shirt, so are you."

"I've never slept with a shirt on." He raises a hand to run the backs of his fingers across my collarbone, the hollow of my throat, and down my breastbone, making me shiver. "I know you've noticed."

Of course, I notice. It was a stupid thing to say, but I'm standing here topless while he's fully dressed. "It's late. I need to get ready for bed."

"You're skipping your ridiculous ritual tonight."

"No, I have to—"

"You're fucking gorgeous, Laynee." He stands, reaches behind his head, and yanks off his shirt. "And it has nothing to do with that shit you put on your face."

His hands drop to the button on his jeans, drawing my attention to the taut abs on display. He unzips, shoves down the denim, and kicks it away. The tight black briefs leave little to the imagination, and his unruly hair looks sexier now than it did when he styled it this morning.

I have to avert my eyes to focus on what he said. "I'm forty years old, Decker. If I skip my beauty regime—"

"You'll still be the second hottest woman in existence."

The second? A smile pulls at my lips. "Who's the first?"

"Megan Fox," he says in a tone that blows past *of course* and goes straight to *facepalm*.

"Yeah, Megan's a sweetheart. She's also married.

They've been together since she was eighteen." I sigh. "When he's not riding her coattails, he's holding her back from her career. It's a shame."

"You don't have a very high opinion of men."

"There's a lot of assholes in my industry."

"You know…" His fingers curl around mine. "I was teasing you about Megan Fox."

"You don't have to say that. I'm not—"

"I mean it. You have a classy, vivacious kind of beauty that no one can mimic. The kind of beauty that turns me into an idiot every time I look at you."

His compliment hits me in the knees. Why does he have to be so nice? He's thoughtful and charming and impossible to resist.

So was Blake. Until he got what he wanted from me—a successful career. What's Decker's motivation?

Your smile. Your body. Rigorous, mutually-pleasurable, savage sex.

If sex with me is his incentive, what will he do after he gets it?

The scars on my back twinge at the thought.

He circles behind me and rests his hands on my hips. "I'm going to remove your jeans." Hovering his mouth over my shoulder, he breathes against my neck. "I'll let you keep the panties on…*tonight*."

Goosebumps race up my spine, and I grab the hands inching toward my fly. "Wait."

"Laynee." His voice is deep and measured, stroking all my pleasure centers. "I know I said no questions, but I need to ask." He presses a kiss to my shoulder. "Were you attacked from the front or the back?"

I close my eyes, grateful he can't see the shame contorting my face. "The front."

"So when I'm facing you and wrapping my arms around your back..."

"It can be a trigger. Sometimes." I stare at my feet, breathing through the crushing handicap of my emotions. "Not always."

"Okay." Remaining behind me, he unbuttons my fly and hooks his thumbs beneath the waistband.

My pulse quickens. "I need to at least moisturize my face."

I need to escape the seductive heat of his chest against my back, the drugging scent of his masculinity, and the confident fingers dipping into my pants. But when I pull away, he yanks me right back.

"If you go in that bathroom, you won't come out for an hour. I'll get the fucking lotion." He wriggles my jeans down my hips and stops to spread his hands over my lace-covered butt cheeks. "Jesus, your ass is incredible. Standing here in your panties and all those scars, you look like a badass warrior princess."

I laugh, because it's just so...unexpected. *He* is unexpected.

After he removes my jeans, he drops a kiss on my neck and heads to the bathroom with a gait that's so fundamentally male and powerful. He's impeccably built, from the breadth of his shoulders and the inverted *V* of his back to his tight ass and sinewy calves. After training with him for a month on the wrestling mats, I've become achingly familiar with every muscular inch of his body.

When he disappears beyond the doorway, I sit cross-legged on my side of the bed and hold the covers against my chest. He returns a moment later, carrying a bottle of body lotion.

"That's not facial moisturizer." I tuck the sheet

beneath my arms, wearing it like a bath towel.

He stares at the label in confusion. "It's *lotion*."

For dry elbows. It'll probably clog my pores and give me acne, but whatever. He fetched it for me when he could've been a dick about it. I hold out my hand, silently asking for the bottle.

"Lie back." He kneels on the mattress beside me and squirts a dollop on his fingers.

"You're going to do it?" Another laugh escapes my lips. When was the last time I laughed this much?

"Yes. Why is that so funny?"

"I don't know." Grinning, I lower to my back and hold the sheet to my chest. "Have you ever done this before?"

"Can't be any different than applying sun lotion." He catches the grimace on my face. "I've never put any kind of lotion on a woman." He leans over me, straddles one of my thighs, and smears the cream across my forehead, down the bridge of my nose, and on my cheeks. "Your jealousy turns me on."

"I'm not jealous."

With a smirk, he wipes the lotion across my lips. When the chemical taste hits my tongue, I spit it out and burst into laughter because he's laughing, and holy hell, I love that deep rumbling sound. We continue to laugh for no reason at all, and eventually drift into shared smiles and heavy breaths. I'm suddenly hyper-aware of the knee denting the mattress between my legs.

The air around us stirs as the mood changes and intensifies. His rapt attention on my face dries my throat. His unwavering attention holds me in place, and his body, while unnaturally still, seems to be sinking on top of me, his weight growing heavier by the second.

His gaze lifts to my forehead and returns to my

eyes. I wet my lips. His face dips lower, his focus skipping to my cheeks, my nose, and back to my eyes. He's staring but seems distracted by…

"The lotion isn't rubbed in, is it?" I touch my brow.

"Not even a little."

I don't care, as long as he continues to look at me like this. Like I mean something beyond a paycheck or an orgasm.

He pushes my hand away and gently massages the cream into my skin, his fingers skimming around my eyes, along my jaw, and tracing my lips.

My eyes drift closed as I imagine doing normal things with him, such as shopping for groceries, going to a rock concert, and stealing kisses while waiting in line at a Starbucks.

I long for any of those scenarios. Could he be the one to share those things with? I feel myself latching on. Physically—with my fingers digging into his shoulders. Emotionally—with the every tha'thunk of my heart.

It's happening. I'm already obsessing, and I haven't even let him in. I can't do this. Not again.

Uncontrollable fear swamps my chest, and I shove at him. When he doesn't move, the sensation of smothering constricts my lungs and chokes my breaths.

He grabs my wrists. "What are you—?"

I go berserk, flailing and swinging and fighting for air. "Get off me!"

"Laynee, stop." He releases my hands and straddles my hips, trapping me. "You're reacting and not thinking."

"Get off. Get off." I wheeze and slap at his chest. "I can't breathe."

"Laynee, goddammit. Remember what I taught

you." He grips my jaw, forcing my gaze to his. "Make space, shrimp, bridge, and roll. We've done this a hundred times."

Shit, he's right. He fucking drilled it into my head for a month.

With a shredded breath, I lift my butt off the mattress and distribute my weight on the balls of my feet and my shoulders. Snapping my legs straight, I shoot out from beneath him. My body bends at the waist, and my rear end lands where my shoulders were.

I did it! I'm so ecstatic about escaping his weight, I forget to bridge and roll until it's too late.

He grabs my leg and yanks me back under him. "You have to follow through. Do it again."

Clenching my hands, I repeat the technique, and this time, when he reaches for me, I've rolled far enough away to make a run for it.

But I don't have to run. *He's not the enemy.*

"Good girl." He sits back on his heels, looking way too naked and chiseled to be in my bed.

"I panicked." I press my back against the headboard and drag the sheet over my chest. "I'll never get that maneuver right in a real-life situation."

"Yes, you will. The rule of thumb is it takes about sixty hours to learn basic self-defense. You're not even halfway there."

I nod, flushed, still panting, and avoid his stare. I can't believe I freaked out like that. If there's a meter for embarrassment, I've reached the ninth level of *curl-up-in-a-hole-and-die.*

"Look at me." His gravelly timbre strokes across my skin.

I ball my hands in the bedding and lift my eyes to his.

He leans forward, resting forearms on his thighs, his shoulders broad and bare and distracting. "Tell me what I did to trigger your panic attack."

"It's not you." I rub my forehead, frustrated and exhausted. "I mean, it's you. You being here. But there's something wrong with me."

He watches me for a moment before moving into the space beside me. Lying on his back, he pulls the sheet over his lower body and pats his chest. "Come here."

Against my better judgment, I long to sleep in his arms, against his warm skin, and he's giving me that instead of demanding answers. Sliding down alongside him, I tuck in against his body with my cheek on his shoulder.

He reaches up and turns off the lamp. With his arm around my back, his fingers roam, seeking and massaging my scars. The gesture produces a burning sensation behind my eyes. Blake pretended my scars didn't exist. I always try to ignore them, too. But I can't. I feel them deep beneath the surface, and Decker's acknowledging them in the best way possible.

"When it happened…" My throat tightens as my voice shatters the dark silence. "I didn't want the press to find out for reasons I don't want to talk about tonight." The shame is more than I can bear. "I had my choice of surgeons. I could've gone to one that would've repaired the damage and prevented scarring. Hell, I can go under the knife now and get them removed. But I chose the surgeon I trusted most. The one who would never sell me out. Unfortunately, he doesn't specialize in cosmetic or plastic surgery."

"I wish you didn't hide them. Instead of walking the red carpet in those obnoxious designer gowns, you should wear your scars like precious gems. Now that would be stunning."

"The court of public opinion wouldn't agree." I stretch my fingers across his hard stomach and trace the dents and bumps of his abs. "It would ruin my career."

"Fuck them. Your body tells a story—an honest one full of trauma and bravery and *survival.* A story you're going to share with me tomorrow, even if I have to spank it out of you. Actually, I'm looking forward to reddening your ass."

"Spanking is a hard limit." My pulse quickens, despite the unbidden grin that twitches my cheeks.

"I feel your smile." He brushes my hair behind my ear and touches the corner of my mouth. "Tell me where *you* feel it."

"What do you mean?"

He kisses the top of my head. "When you smile, do you feel it in your cheeks? Your veins? Your pussy? Where do you feel happy?"

"I feel it here." I clasp his hand and place it over my heart.

"That's right." He shifts closer, scooting down to eye-level with his body facing mine. "All of this…" He sweeps a hand down my back. "And this." His finger taps my smile. "And this." He cups me between the legs, over my panties. "It's all an illustration of what's going on here." His hand returns to my chest. "Sometimes all you need is a shift in perspective, and everything on the outside will change with it."

"Wow." I brush my fingers through his hair, lost in his words and the glow of his eyes in the dark. "When did you become so philosophical?"

"When I found out my best friend is a pedophile." He touches his forehead to mine. "Bad shit happens to everyone. We all hurt. We all struggle. But only the strong will heal. Those who have support and patience and indomitable spirit. When you heal, Laynee, you'll wear your scars with pride."

CHAPTER 15

I wake to a warm, delicious pressure stroking between my legs. Languid and groggy, I open my thighs and arch into the blissful sensation. I love when he rouses me from sleep with his lips, his fingers, and his hard cock. He must've been touching me for a while, because I'm already primed, trembling, feverish, and wet.

"Trey," I moan.

The caress vanishes, and mattress bounces beside me.

"What did you say?"

That voice.

My heart stops, and my eyes flash open. The dark shadow sitting up on the bed is too big to be Trey. The voice is too deep and calm.

I yank the sheet up my body and try to clear my head. I'm in Savannah, not L.A. I'm with a man who's never hurt me. This isn't a dream that ends in a nightmare. At least, I hope not. I hope I didn't just screw everything up.

Falling asleep in Decker's arms last night was a momentous step for me. I hadn't done that with anyone in years. Not even with Blake. Not since Trey. Trey's the only lover I ever truly trusted. Is that why I was thinking about him?

"I'm sorry." I reach for Decker's rigid shoulder.

He catches my wrist and holds it in the coil of heat between us. "Who the fuck is Trey? Another ex-husband?"

My chest squeezes. "You said no questions."

He roughly releases my arm and shoves off the bed.

"Where are you going?" I lift to my knees, panicky and aroused and burning up with shame.

"I'm going to take care of this." He flips on the bathroom light, turns sideways in the doorway, and gestures at his groin.

The glow behind his silhouette throws his profile into stark relief, cutting a long hard outline around the erection tenting his briefs.

"Come back. Please." Every nerve-ending in my body fires to life, energizing me with courage. "I want to watch you."

He stares at me from across the dark room, lowers his hand, and begins to stroke the huge swell in his briefs. "You know what I want?"

"What?" My whisper sounds like a croak.

"I want to know who Trey is. Tell me that, and I'll let you watch."

My hands fist in the bedding. I force my fingers to relax and my lips to move. "He's the one I was with before Blake."

"Six years ago?"

"Yeah." My stomach twists.

He prowls back to the bed and switches on the lamp. "Where is he now?"

I close my eyes. Decker's already figured out that I trusted the person who tried to kill me. My silence will only make this worse.

Dragging my gaze to his, I blink, swallow, and

blink again. "Trey's dead."

And I just called out his name while Decker was touching me. If Decker didn't know I was fucked up, he certainly knows now.

I brace myself for a barrage of questions and judgment. But he remains eerily quiet as he reclines on his back beside me and bends an arm behind his head. His other hand lifts the elastic of his briefs, stretching it over his stiff cock and down his legs.

My mouth goes dry, and my pulse howls in my ears. Holy fuck, his cock is beautiful. Long and thick, it defies gravity and pulses in the lamp light. The plump head beads with pre-come, and his balls sit enticingly in the cradle of his powerful thighs. If I sat on that thing, I'd definitely feel it.

I'd feel it for days.

Lifting my gaze, I find a lazy grin on his stunning face. Those sleepy eyes, plump lips, and coarse stubble—all the lineaments of his expression look stronger, hungrier, in the backdrop of that grin.

"You're such a sexy bastard," I whisper. "I bet you hear that all the time, don't you?"

His arrogant smile tips sideways. "Touch me." He kicks off the underwear and curls his fingers around his girth. "My chest, my cock… I don't care where. Just put your hands on me."

I kneel beside him and slide my palms over the compact ripples of his abs. He's a masterpiece of flesh and steel. All hard lines, heavy muscle, and taut skin.

I peer into his hooded eyes and let him see my appreciation. But when the smacking sound of his fist fills the room, I'm drawn to it, hypnotized by the sight of this strong, virile man stroking himself into mindless pleasure.

"How many times have you done this since you've been here?" I skim my hands lower, tracing the trimmed patch of hair at the base of his cock.

"Every day. Multiple times a day." He twists his wrist, fucking his fist with confident familiarity. "Do you touch yourself, Laynee?"

"Every day since I met you." In the shower. In my office. Anywhere I can sneak away. I drift closer, and my nipples graze his chest. "You make me crazy, Decker."

He groans, and his hand moves faster. "Give me that sinful mouth."

I lower to my hip, stretch across his torso, and press my lips to his. His mouth lifts, hungry and hot, his tongue whipping as aggressively as the fist on his cock. He devours me with an urgency and fever that melts my insides and steals my air. I become consciously aware of the nerves beneath my skin, the muscles spasming between my legs, and the pull of my heart as it rips from my chest.

"Are you wet?" He nips at my lips.

"Yes." I lean back to watch his hand glide erotically, furiously, up and down that gorgeous cock.

"Sit on my face."

I moan with longing, a weakness that never ends well for me. "I like to watch." Watching is safer.

"Sit with your back to the headboard." He moves his free hand to join the other, widening his legs to play with his balls as he strokes himself. "I'll keep my hands on my dick, and you can watch while I eat your pussy."

My pussy throbs, rushing me toward climax just from his words.

"If you don't fucking move," he says, panting through harsh breaths, "I'm going to finish in the bathroom. Alone."

Shit. "You drive a hard bargain, Decker Gabrielli."

He half-laughs, half-groans. "Says the woman who negotiates sex."

His reminder about the deal I offered should give me pause. I avoid intimacy for a reason, but in my lust-crazed haze, I can't remember what that reason is.

Rising to my knees, I shift toward his head.

"The panties." His eyes blaze with dark fire. "Take them off."

I remove them quickly, shove the pillow away, and straddle his face with my back to the headboard. As I start to lower, he groans.

"Wait." His hands still, one squeezing the root of his cock, the other cupping his balls. "I want to look for a second."

My inner muscles clench, and I wonder if he can see it. This is such a vulnerable position with his eyes inches from my most private part, taking me in and forming opinions. I imagine most of his lovers are in their early twenties, half my age, and a whole lot tighter…everywhere. The urge to roll away bunches my shoulders.

"Pink and swollen and perfect." He turns his head and nips at the inside of my thigh. "You're so fucking wet you're dripping down your legs." His cock jerks his hand. "Lower that ass. I need to taste you."

The stroke of his hand resumes, faster, harder, his knuckles blanching around his length. I lower toward his mouth and rest my palms on his chest, relishing the feel of flexing muscle and sparse hair beneath my fingers. My legs spread wide in the awkward position—awkward only because his shoulders are so broad and his biceps are bouncing against the insides of my knees as he works his cock.

The moment my pussy touches his lips, he groans. I gasp and lift up. But his mouth chases, locks on with diabolical suction, and his tongue slides through my folds.

"Ohhhh, fuck!" My head falls back. My legs weaken, and my entire body liquefies.

I sink against his mouth, my ribs expanding with indrawn breaths and my fingers curling against his chest. He mumbles something, his lips strong and firm, drawing every thought and sensation to the center of my body where he unfurls a maddening ripple of ecstasy with his tongue.

When he groans again, garbling his words, I raise slightly to hear him.

"You taste so damn good. I need you to grind." He bites my thigh, harder this time. "Hurry. I'm barely hanging on, and I'm not coming until you do."

My gaze travels down the length of his twitching body. Every brick of muscle is engaged. A sheen of perspiration forms on his skin. And his cock…that gorgeous swell of flesh and blood looks painfully choked in the shackle of his hand.

I've been carrying around so much sexual tension over the past month it feels like a pressure-cooker inside me. My limbs are loose. My skin is fevered, and my pussy's gushing with arousal. So as I relax all my weight and begin to grind, my orgasm grips me instantly, brutally, and without warning. I come so fucking hard I scream without breath, every muscle in my body shaking with the explosion.

His hand loses rhythm, jerking once, twice, his legs and arms shaking. A long deep moan vibrates against my overstimulated tissues, and I lift just in time to hear it morph into a guttural shout.

"Fuck, Laynee. Fuuuuuck!" His body goes rigid, and ropes of come stream over his hand and abs.

I tremble at the glorious sight and roll to his side, boneless and fighting for air. He climbs over me, mouth parted, chest heaving, and attacks my mouth. The tangy flavor of my arousal slides over my tongue as he kisses me hard and deep, with no less passion than before his release.

Without breaking the kiss, he slips a hand between us and wipes the semen from his stomach. Then he spreads it across mine, up my chest, and around my throat. It's the most erotic thing I've ever experienced.

His lips ghost along my jaw and dip to my neck, lingering there before lowering to my breast.

"Why did you do that?" I arch beneath the swirl of his tongue against my nipple.

"What? This?" He swipes at a white smear on my chest and slips his fingers into my mouth.

I lick the salty essence from his skin and briefly close my eyes. "Yeah, that."

His hand combs through my hair, and his dark eyes fill my view. "I've fantasized about coming on your beautiful skin…among a hundred other things." He kisses my lips. "We should go back to sleep or those other things are going to happen tonight." He glances at the clock. *2:23 AM.* "Today." He flashes a grin that turns me into shivery mush.

"Come on." He rolls back onto his side of the bed and turns off the light. Straightening the pillows, he stretches out on his back and taps his chest. "Get your sexy ass over here."

Covered in his come, I feel dirty and tired and fucked in the best way possible. And that's what worries me, but I'll save that worry for later. Right now, I want nothing more than to be a normal woman, sleeping in the arms of a man who cares about me.

Once I'm in the position he wants, with my body curled around his and my head tucked beneath his chin, he says, "I'm going to L.A. with you tomorrow."

We've been arguing about this trip for a few days. For whatever reason, he doesn't want me to go without him.

"I've been talking to your security team." He strokes a hand through my hair. "I'll stand in as one of your bodyguards. No one will know about our relationship."

Our relationship. Those words fill me with both longing and dread. "What's your motivation to go with me?" I recall something he said in passing about opening another combat sports school. "Are you hoping to cozy up with my contacts and pitch your business ventures?"

"Yes."

I stiffen as my old insecurities flood in.

"Laynee." He pulls me closer against his body. "If I meet someone who's interested in me, it could be the break I'm looking for."

Blake said those exact words, and I was too stupid in lust to understand he was using me. Hell, I pulled every string I had to launch his career in Hollywood.

"But that's not why I'm going." He lifts on an elbow and stares down at me, his face cast in shadows. "I'm your partner, your companion, *your lover*. Your security team is qualified, but they're not *me*. I can't sit here with my thumb up my ass while you're on the other side of the country, being stalked by creepers, hounded by paparazzi, and sleeping in a hotel room alone. You're not going without me."

For all my cynical distrust, his response makes my chest swell with happiness. Makes me wonder if he's capable of loving someone as messed up as me. Makes me hope for a life that's safely and forever entwined with his.

I pull in a breath and shake those thoughts away. "Violet called earlier."

"I know. I was there when you walked out on our conversation to take the call."

"I'm sorry. That was rude. But you'll like what she had to say."

"She said you're not to leave my side? Ever?"

My cheeks fill with a grin. "Close. Evidently, I'm doing a terrible job at proving I've moved on from Blake."

"You haven't left the house in a month."

"Yeah, she expresses her frustration about that on a daily basis. She can't keep me at the top of the news stories if I refuse interviews and public appearances and blah, blah, blah."

"I've enjoyed having you all to myself."

I've enjoyed that, too. *Too much.* "She wants you to go to L.A."

"Good thing, since I'm going anyway."

"She wants you to go as my boyfriend."

CHAPTER 16

Laynee

The roar of the jet engines taper to a dull hum as we reach coasting altitude. I stare out the small window, absorbing the majestic beauty of the sunrise over Savannah. At my request, Reese sat in the rear of my sixteen-passenger Gulfstream with the bodyguards, leaving me alone with the man who hasn't taken his eyes off me since we boarded.

"Why are you staring?" I turn to face Decker's smoldering gaze.

Sitting in the aisle seat beside me, he places a hand on my knee. "Can't stop thinking about last night." His thumb lightly strokes the skin beneath my skirt. "And this morning."

My body's still wired and vibrating after he followed me into the shower this morning, knelt at my feet, and buried his face between my legs. I came with my hands tangled in his hair and his name on my lips. Then he washed us both and rushed us out the door without finding his own release.

I rest my hand over his and weave our fingers together. "I owe you an orgasm."

"I'll collect before the end of the day."

"I don't see how. Today is going to be a whirlwind."

The five-hour flight puts us in L.A. by eleven in

the morning. The photo shoot will last a few hours, and because I refuse to stay overnight in L.A., we're flying back home when the shoot is finished.

"Let me worry about that." He slides a thumb over his sexy bottom lip, his eyes dancing with promises. "Why are you doing this photo shoot?"

He already knows it's for a magazine spread, a promo opportunity that highlights the top hottest Hollywood bachelorettes. I'm the oldest of the four selected women by fifteen years. I fought doing this for months, but my agent and publicist won the argument. They're right. It's perfect timing on the heels of my divorce announcement.

"When the glossy goes to print," I say, "it'll shine a favorable light on my single status and in turn redirect focus on the mysterious man I'm dating. It's all part of the sweep-my-divorce-under-the-rug strategy."

"I like being your mysterious man." He leans over, brushes my long hair behind me, and touches his nose to my neck, inhaling. "Goddamn, I love the way you smell."

My breath catches. "What do I smell like?"

"Sweet, bite-sized temptation." He pushes the collar of my blouse aside and nibbles on my throat. "Why don't we stay the night in L.A.?"

The desire he's igniting with his lips quickly dissolves with his question.

I sent Reese to the rear of the plane so I could use this time to give Decker some answers. He just gave me an opening, and my voice decides to abandon me.

"Laynee." He lifts his head, and the concern in his huge brown eyes latches on to my heart. "You're squeezing the circulation out of my fingers."

Oh. I release his hand and turn my head toward

the clouds outside the plane. "We need to talk."

"Are you addressing me or the window?"

I drop my head back and close my eyes, unable to meet the gaze caressing the side of my face. "This...*us*...I'm going to mess it up."

"Tell me why you think that."

Where to start? "I try too hard. Or maybe I don't try hard enough. Men like the idea of me. The stardom and the money. But when I let someone in and he gets to know me, something happens. He becomes cruel. Hateful." *Abusive.* "But by then, I'm already attached."

He grips my knee, his hand a warm heavy support. "That's on them, Laynee."

I shake my head and twist my fingers together on my lap. I have no right to take advantage of his patience, but the sharp pang in my chest is crippling. It takes several minutes to gather my thoughts and turn to face him.

"I have a void in my life. It's always been there. The thing about being the only child of famous parents is that this void went unnoticed in my otherwise envious upbringing and lifestyle. I've always had money and stability and opportunities. My parents loved me, provided for me, and I lacked for nothing. *Except their time.*"

He squeezes my knee, urging me to continue.

I pull in a deep breath. "I didn't have their attention. I was never as important as their public image and career aspirations. In fact, I wasn't really on their radar. They spent my entire childhood on movie sets in different parts of the world while I grew up in Savannah with the hired help. My closest relationships consisted of a few dozen nannies and some superficial friendships at school. My peers weren't from

Hollywood, so they were much more interested in my celebrity connections than getting to know me." I laugh hollowly. "It took years of therapy for me to come to terms with all this."

He removes his seatbelt, unfastens mine, and drags me onto his lap. The gesture startles me, but I welcome it, settling against his chest with my head on his shoulder.

"I swear I'm not whining about my privileged life." Kicking off my heels, I rest my bare feet on the seat I vacated. "I feel extremely fortunate for everything I have. But that void in my childhood, my lack of close relationships… It created a deep hole inside me."

"Loneliness." He cups my face, tucking my head beneath his chin. "That's what you feel?"

"Yeah. I tend to force connections with men, connections that don't exist. I deepen relationships that aren't meant to be. I find love in little crumbs of affection, and I make excuses when those men hurt me." I shift to look into his eyes. "When someone wonderful comes along and shows me a glimpse of kindness, I get attached. But at the same time, I don't trust him, because I know his interest in me isn't genuine. I know it won't last."

"Not all men are useless pieces of shit."

"That's exactly what I tell myself every time I meet someone." I give him a pointed look. It terrifies me, but I really do trust Decker. "Trey McCree wasn't my first bad decision, but he was by far the worst."

"How did you meet him?" Decker slides a hand over the scars on my back.

I tilt my head and listen for a moment. A low din of voices drifts from the back seats, too far away to make out words. That means my security team can't hear our conversation.

"I met him in a L.A. bar, of all places. It was a night of terrible decisions. I just came out of a bad breakup. I had an obsessed stalker on the loose. I sneaked away from my bodyguard, went to a bar, alone, wearing a disguise. I just wanted to be a normal woman for one night and hookup with a normal man. I connected with Trey instantly and went home with him."

Decker's entire body stiffens beneath me. "Is that when he tried to kill you?"

"No." I'd be able to forgive myself if that were the case. "We spent the next six months together, inseparable and happy. He was wholly invested in *me*. He didn't give a shit about my name or my money. He was protective, possessive, and ferociously jealous. I have a weakness for dominant men, and I thought his overbearing need to control me meant he loved me."

Decker remains completely still against me. I'm not even sure he's breathing.

"He moved in with me." My voice weakens with remembered pain. "His jealousy grew darker, uglier. I was filming *Angel of Fear* at the time, and there were numerous love scenes. I didn't use a body double back then, and Trey… He did *not* approve. We argued about it endlessly, and the words that came out of his mouth…" My throat tightens. "His words were familiar."

"What do you mean?" he asks in a low, deep tone.

"I started receiving more and more menacing letters from that stalker. The notes obsessed over my relationships with other men, threatening to kill me if I took my clothes off with my costar or if I spent time alone with Elijah, who was my only bodyguard at the time. Not once did the letters mention my boyfriend, and every word was horribly similar to things Trey said when we fought. I started piecing it together."

"Trey was your stalker." Decker's fingers clench and release against my back.

My chin trembles. "I asked him about it. Of course, he denied it, but I knew. He approached me at that bar because he was already stalking me." A surge of grief burns through my chest and pricks the backs of my eyes. "I knew he was the stalker and told no one. Not Reese or Elijah or the PI I hired."

"Because you loved the son of a bitch," Decker growls.

"I thought I did. I thought I could handle him. I thought he loved me too much to hurt me. I thought wrong."

He grips the back of my blouse, pulls it from the skirt, and glides his palm across my scarred skin. "You don't have to tell me any more."

"I need to." I relax against his warm touch and close my eyes. "It happened the night of the premier of *Angel of Fear*. Reese and Trey went to the viewing with me. After, Reese dropped us off at home. Trey was quiet but affectionate when he took me to bed. He…" I cover my mouth to stifle the sudden break in my voice. "He kissed me, fucked me. It was rougher than usual. I don't know where the knife came from. I didn't even know he was holding it while he was…f-fucking me." A sob rises up, and my hands shake against the onslaught of memory.

Decker crushes me against his chest, shushing me, but the tension in his muscles suggests he's struggling to rein in his anger.

"I fought him." Tears leak from my eyes and wet my voice. "But it happened so fast, and he was bigger, stronger, and armed." I suck in a breath. "I'm alive because Reese came back to the house to return my phone. I'd left it in his car. He heard my screams. Grabbed the gun I kept in my office. Trey fled before Reese fired off a shot."

"You said Trey was dead?"

"He died two weeks later in a car crash in Texas." I straighten on his lap and let him see the words I'm not saying.

He searches my face, and his brown eyes widen. "You hired—?"

I press a hand over his mouth and glance toward the rear of the plane. Only Reese and Elijah know the details.

Twining my arms around his neck, I touch my forehead to his temple. "We didn't call the cops that night. Didn't involve law enforcement at all. Reese took me to the one surgeon I trusted, an old friend of my father's. As for Trey… I had him hunted down and removed from the face of the Earth, efficiently and quietly."

"Thank fuck." His hand curls around my waist. "I'd hate to miss out on *this*"—he squeezes my hip—"because I'm serving time for killing that motherfucker." His tone softens. "Thank you for trusting me enough to tell me."

My breaths catch in my chest. Did I do the right thing? Or have I fallen into another lovesick trap?

"Why didn't you involve the cops?" he asks.

"Shame." I touched the sudden hardness in his jaw. "I let my stalker move in with me and embed himself in my life. If that story is ever leaked, it'll ruin me. I never even told Blake how I got the scars. Our marriage was doomed from the beginning, because I never trusted him with that secret. Never trusted him not to hurt me with it. As it turns out, my distrust was justified. He slept with every starlet he worked with, as well as my housekeeper and female bodyguards. Each time I confronted him about it, he beat the shit out of me."

"He *what?*" Decker surges to the edge of the seat, his arms locking around me to keep me from falling.

"I'm messed up, Decker. I can't even stay the night in L.A. because I'm haunted by memories of the relationships I had there." Placing my hands on his chest, I nudge him back into the leather recliner. "I make awful choices when it comes to men. That's why I let Reese choose my lovers, and why I turned to Infidelity. *They* selected you. That alone gives me hope. Though I specifically requested a submissive man, and you're—"

"You don't want a submissive." He grips my jaw. "You want a man you can trust. The two are not related." He releases my face, his expression contemplative. "Your cheating ex-husband needs a fucking beat down. One he won't walk away from."

"Decker—"

"He's the reason you don't have a housekeeper?"

I nod. "And why my bodyguards are all men. Except Rachel."

"Your chauffeur…" He angles his head toward the back, spotting Rachel among the men. "She's a bodyguard?"

"And a lesbian." I give him a small smile. "If you make a pass at her, she'll shoot you."

His chest rises and falls, and he reclines deeper

into the seat, taking me with him. His fingers find my hair, stroking from roots to tips over and over, spreading a comforting tingle across my scalp. I threw a lot of shit at him, and instead of pushing him for his thoughts on it all, I surrender to his touch, relax against his chest, and close my eyes. Just as I begin to drift off, his hand stops its hypnotic caress.

"I'm going to fuck you," he says quietly but firmly. "Before the day is over."

My stomach hardens, and I lift my head. "Only if Reese—"

He grips my hair, holding my cheek against his shoulder and his mouth at my ear. "You think putting Reese in our bed will keep things casual and safe?" His fingers flex, pulling at the roots of my hair, his voice grinding with anger. "We missed our opportunity for casual sex the night we met. After the trust you've given me, the intensity burning through every touch we share, and all the emotions we haven't even vocalized yet, *nothing* will ever be casual between us. So get that idea out of your stubborn head. Whether you like it or not, I'm one-hundred-percent invested in us."

"Why?" I break his hold to meet his eyes. "You've never committed to a woman. Why is this any different?"

"I don't know." His eyebrows pull together, and his gaze traces my face. "Maybe because I went into this mentally prepared to commit to you for a year."

My chest pinches. He's invested in the Infidelity agreement. Of course, that's all this is.

"I've never slept beside a woman," he says. "I've never enjoyed spending time with a woman I'm not fucking. I've never had to chase a woman so hard and for so goddamn long." He flashes a huge grin, as if chasing me excites him. "And I've never felt this…this…" He shoves a hand through his hair and looks away. "I feel anxious and sick when I'm not near you."

That'll wear off. Probably as soon as he fucks me. Then he'll hurt me. Not physically. Maybe not even with words. But my heart's on the table, right there for the taking. The more time I spend with him, the less I'm able to protect it. Someday, he'll break it, and this time, I'm not sure I'll heal.

Chapter 17

Laynee

The photographers and production crew bustle around the massive room, adjusting lighting and furniture. I lean against the wall on the far side, wearing a relaxed smile. It's the smile I use in public to make me appear demure and content, when all I really want to do is go home.

I used to love L.A., the diversity of ethnicity and wealth, the microclimate of urban heat, and the way the sun illuminates the motley of neighborhoods in a unified glow. It's the city of dreamers. But when I left two years ago, I was no longer chasing the dream. I was running from a nightmare.

Shutting the door on those thoughts, I look around the room. *Where the hell is Decker?*

When we arrived at the studio, he stayed with my security detail while the stylists whisked me into the dressing room. That was two hours ago. I haven't seen him since.

Shifting my weight from one leg to the other, I try to ease the cramps in my feet caused by the strappy five-inch stilettos. My face itches beneath the heavy makeup and frozen smile, and my scars tingle under the Victoria Beckham form-fitting dress.

It's been months since I put myself in the spotlight. While I loathe the scrutiny, I know this is good for me. This is the life I chose.

The three celebrity bachelorettes I'm posing with today gather a few feet away, droning on about shopping, spa treatments, and the hottest nightclubs in L.A. They sample the fruit selections on the refreshments table, taking delicate bites and tossing uneaten portions in the trash.

Dressed buoyantly and seductively in designer fabrics, they're beautiful, successful, and at least fifteen years younger than me. If any one of them stepped outside, men would trip over themselves to get a closer look. If they walked out together, they would cause a riot.

"...is intravenous vitamin therapy." Alley Fahy, best known for her roles in romantic comedies, points her famous button nose in my direction. "Don't you agree, Laynee?"

"I wasn't following the conversation." I smooth my damp palms down the shiny material of my dress.

The wardrobe stylist said the color of the dress is cerulean blue, chosen to match my eyes. I told her the hem's too short for a forty-year-old woman. It covers my scars but fits like a tennis skirt. She told me not to bend over and shooed me away.

"Apple stem cell facials are all the rage." Alley tilts her auburn head. "Better results than vitamin therapy, right?"

I shrug. I've tried it all. "I swear by healthy eating habits and daily moisturizer." *Especially when the moisturizer is applied with strong masculine fingers.*

"But at your age, you have to do so much more." Her gaze flicks to my chest. "Ever considered augmentation?"

Resisting the urge to hug my torso, I hold my

arms at my sides and widen my smile. "No. Never."

The youngest of the group, Collette Conway, leans toward Alley and mumbles, "She might've hung on to Blake Harridan a little longer if she had some of that lifted and tucked."

"Really, Collette?" I swallow a furious rush of air and temper my voice. "We were doing so good there, behaving professionally and amicably like grownups. Why did you have to ruin it by being a dick?"

Collette's shoulders snap back, and a scowl warps her pretty elfin features.

"We're just trying to help," Alley says in a bored tone as she adjusts the string of diamonds on her wrist. "You're not a spring chicken, Laynee, and now you're divorced. If you don't upgrade your appearance, you'll end your career as a tired old maid."

Outrage spikes through my veins, but the actress in me maintains a regal smile. "If you don't upgrade your personality, you'll end your career as a hollow plastic bitch."

She inhales sharply. "Is that a threat?"

I'd give her a nasty look, but she already has one. "If you think I'm so tired and old, how about you fight me?" I bat my eyelashes and grin. "After the photo shoot, you and I can have a little sparring match and find out how well your implants stand up to my fists."

A month ago, I would've never proposed such a thing. But after training with Decker, I'm confident enough to take on a scrawny skank. Sadly, I don't think Alley takes my offer seriously.

"You're insane." Her attention locks on something across the room, and she clutches Collette's wrist. "Oh. My. God."

The trio of women turn toward the sudden

activity at the back entrance. Reese and two of my bodyguards veer off to the side, but the women remain fixated on the door and the man who just walked in.

Decker's sharp gaze scans the crew of people darting around the crowded studio. Dark denim stretches across his powerful thighs and sits low on his hips. A white collared shirt hangs off his shoulders, unbuttoned and exposing a gray undershirt molded around defined pecs. The black studded belt, worn Converse, and tousled hair gives him the rebellious look I find so damn irresistible.

"Who the hell is he?" Alley whispers. "I've never seen anything that hot. Jesus."

"He must be a model." Collette absently runs a hand over her black hair. "Look at those biceps. And eyes. Dear God, his lips."

"I don't know who he is," Alley says breathlessly. "But I saw him first. He's mine."

My molars crash together. It's going to crush me when he smiles at them. It'll destroy me if he flirts with them. They're young and stunning and preening like peacocks in anticipation of his attention. With just one of his roguish winks, he could have all three of them in bed. At the same time.

Except he signed an agreement, and I paid a handsome amount of money for his commitment. He's stuck with me for eleven more months.

I push down my stupid insecurities and watch him from beneath my lashes as he surveys the room.

His proud posture exudes swagger and sex as he rests his fingertips in the front pockets of his jeans. The catty women beside me aren't the only ones stunned into speechless ogling. The male crew members stare and give him a wide berth. The female technicians steal glances, their hands fumbling with equipment as they dare another peek.

His complexion is golden from our morning jogs on the trails, and his brown eyes shimmer in the glow of a nearby light modifier. It's impossible not to stare at him. He's an erotic work of art, hotter than hot, and he knows it.

His dark eyes pan left to right, and when they lock on me, a wicked grin spreads across his face. I melt against the wall at my back.

Holding my gaze, he heads in my direction, his long-legged strides eating up the distance and sending my pulse into a soaring spiral.

"Holy shit." Alley straightens in my periphery. "He's coming this way."

With each step, his eyes become clearer, more intense, never leaving mine. I can't breathe or move or look away. I'm utterly gobsmacked by his unwavering focus on me.

"It's criminal how good-looking he is," Collette whispers under her breath. "I want to lick him. Every. Hard. Fuckable. Inch."

A possessive thrill shoots through me. I sleep beside that man every night. I've seen the way his naked body flexes as he fucks his hand, and I've come all over those delicious lips. Twice.

I might not have been his first choice in a companion, but he hasn't taken his eyes off me once to check out the women at my side. He could be doing it out of respect for my public image or simply because he likes looking at me. Regardless of the reason, it makes my heart beat a joyful dance against my ribs. He's gone way past his obligation to make me feel special, attractive, secure. *Claimed.*

Ten feet away, his gaze breaks from mine to browse my body. It's an unhurried trip that lingers on my chest, my bare legs, and the short hem of my dress, before returning to my eyes.

"Damn." He rubs his clean-shaved jaw, his mouth tipping in a panty-melting smile. "You're unbelievably—"

"Hey there, gorgeous." Alley leans against the wall beside me. "Got a name?"

"Yep." His eyes hold mine, gleaming with mischief and other things. Things meant just for me.

I pin my lips between my teeth.

"We were wondering," Alley says, "if you'd be kind enough to take off your shirt."

He steps into my space, his gaze still fastened to mine, and slides his hands along my jaw, framing my face. "I've been checking in on you. They hogged you in that dressing room for two hours. I didn't like it."

I sway in my heels, transfixed by the lips I want to kiss more than anything and the hooded gaze that falls away to stare at my mouth.

"Are you—?" Alley's voice invades my Decker-drunk fog. "Are you two together?"

His deep brown eyes flash right before he slants his mouth across mine, devouring my sigh. Alley steps away but doesn't go far. I tune out her whispering, close my eyes, and lose myself in his kiss.

With his body flush against mine, he plunders my mouth with an expert tongue, chasing, conquering, and staking his claim. His hand slips beneath my hair to support my neck as the other drops to the back of my thigh, his fingers stretching beneath the skirt to trace the crease between my leg and butt.

The kiss isn't pornographic, but it thrums with

raw sex and urgent need. For whatever reason, he wants me, and he's letting me know with every sinful lick and caress. My hands find his hair as I meet every rub and swirl of his tongue, match each playful bite, and struggle to stay upright.

He tastes the way he smells. Clean, earthy, and elemental, like the atmosphere after a thunderstorm. But he kisses like a hurricane, full of force and fury and devastating power. I want him to sweep me away, damn the consequences.

Too soon, he comes up for air, leaving me wrecked, ravaged, and winded.

He suckles my bottom lip. "Laynee."

"Decker."

"I'm fucking crazy about you."

"You're definitely crazy." I grin.

"I'm going to fuck you in this dress."

A chorus of gasps sounds nearby.

I chuckle against his mouth. "I thought you prefer me bare-faced and wearing yoga pants?"

"Oh, I do, baby. But I'm not gonna lie. Your goddamn legs…" He groans and presses his erection against my hip. "You've given me a huge fucking hard-on."

I'm seconds from blowing off the photo shoot to take care of him when the tread of sneakers hurries toward us.

"No, no, no! Not the lipstick!" The wild-eyed makeup artist shoves him to the side. "What have you done?"

He gives her a withering glare and braces his arms on the wall beside me, keeping his back to the room, presumably to hide his erection. I fight my grin, holding still as the woman repaints my lips.

"No more smudging." She points the lip brush at him, glances at his ass for a beat too long, and marches away.

He moves back in, putting a possessive hand on my hip and a forearm on the wall above my head. The hungry look he gives me makes the room spin. I feel light-headed and reckless and eternally grateful.

With shaky fingers, I wipe the smear of frosted pink gloss from his swollen lips. "Thank you."

"For?"

For not flirting with other women. "For respecting me."

Vertical lines form between his eyebrows. "Is this about the Barbie bookends?"

"The Barbie…?" *Oh.* "Bookends come in pairs." I spot the trio standing a few feet behind him. All slender limbs and glossy hair, they shoot envious venom in my direction. "There's three of them."

"I didn't notice." He touches his forehead to mine. "I'm wearing blinders, Laynee. You're all I see."

Oh, Decker. You know exactly what to say.

I smile wistfully. "What am I going to do with you?"

"Finish your photo shoot, and I'll show you."

CHAPTER 18

Laynee

For the next two hours, the cameras click, the bulbs flash, and my smile strains to the point of pain. When the photography session finally ends, I slip off the heels and carry them toward the dressing room, exhausted to the bone.

Flanked by two of my bodyguards, I reach the hall that leads to the back rooms and find Reese perched on a chair against the wall.

"Hey." He reaches up and squeezes my hand. "You looked stunning out there. I felt sorry for the other girls who had to stand in your shadow."

"You're not biased or anything." I laugh. "But thanks." I peek down the busy hallway. "Where's Decker?"

"I thought he was in the studio. He watched the whole thing."

A wave of warmth floods my chest.

"Maybe he's in the restroom," he says. "Want me to check?"

"That's okay. I'm going to change and wash my face. Then I'll be ready to go."

"The plane's ready when you are."

I reached the door of the dressing room, where one of my security guys stands guard. Call me paranoid, but it's nice to see him here, preventing creepy letters or unwanted visitors from making their way inside.

I lock the door behind me and shuffle toward the vanity and huge lighted mirror, more than ready to get back to Savannah. Resting an elbow on the counter, I reach for the hidden zipper beneath my armpit.

"The dress stays on."

Decker's deep timbre startles a gasp from me, and my gaze jumps to his in the mirror. He prowls toward me, hands behind his back and indecent intent simmering in his eyes.

"I wondered where you went." I straighten, watching him watch my reflection.

"You've been teasing me for hours." He presses up behind me and dips his mouth to my neck.

"Teasing you? I was working."

His hands sweep up the fronts of my thighs and slip under the dress. "I've been staring at your legs along with every other son of a bitch in that room." His thumbs trace the crotch of my panties. "Do you know how cruel that is?" He roughly pulls my butt against the swollen length in his jeans. "It's fucking painful."

I groan at the feel of his hardness against me. "We can't have sex, Decker."

His eyes stay on mine in the mirror as he grabs the front of my panties and yanks hard enough to rip the seams.

The scrap of lace falls down my legs and tangles around my ankles.

I flatten my hands on the counter. "If you fuck me, I'll get attached." *I'm already attached.*

He kisses my neck, his breath hot and seductive. His fingers slide between my legs, slipping deeper and deeper with each wicked stroke through my folds.

With a moan, I let my head tilt to the side, giving him better access. "I'll get needy." *I'm already needy.*

He sinks two fingers into my wetness and gently thrusts his hand. "I'm about to be attached and needy inside your dripping pussy."

His other hand moves to his belt. The clink of the buckle races my pulse. The slide of his zipper quickens my breaths.

"For how long, Decker? What happens at the end of the agreement?" I writhe on the fingers curling inside me, warring with the need to grind against his hand and shove it away. "You'll move on to younger, fresher pastures, and I'll—"

"Shut the fuck up, Laynee."

"If we weren't under a binding legal agreement, I would totally fire you right now."

He bites the back of my dress, pinching the skin beneath, right over the worst of my scars.

With every battered beat of my heart, I know I should tell him to fuck off and end this. But I can't. He gives me exactly what I crave. His dominant position over me makes my blood sing. His cocky personality and powerful body gives me confidence by proxy. And he doesn't pretend my scars don't exist. He forces me to confront them.

I'm not whole on my own, but when I have him at my side, I feel unstoppable. If I let this man put his cock in me, I'll feel connected, loved, complete. I won't ever be able to let go.

His fingers leave my pussy, and clothing rustles behind me. He strips out of both shirts and flips up the skirt of my dress. His gaze drops, lingering on my bare ass for a moment that stretches into several more. His dark eyes flick to my reflection, back to my butt, and he lowers out of view in the mirror.

Without warning, he plunges his fingers into my pussy from behind. I gasp at the burst of pleasure, lifting on my toes and collapsing over the counter of the vanity. He runs his teeth across my ass, nibbling and licking as he fingers me into trembling breathlessness.

"I'm going to fuck you without a condom." He glides his lips downward and buries his mouth between my legs, curling his tongue and pushing me toward that blissful edge. "It'll be a first for me."

I press my heated cheek against the cold counter and try to focus on his words. "You've never had sex without a condom?"

"No." His palm slams against my ass, shooting a stinging fire across my skin.

"What the hell was that for?" I crane my neck to glare at him.

"For making me wait a month for this."

He spanks my other cheek, and the force of it knocks me against the counter, clattering brushes and hair products to the floor.

"Stop!" I pant through the vicious burn, hating that I love the way it turns me on and inside out. "That's a hard limit. No physical pain or—"

His hand collides with my ass three more times in rapid succession. I fight him, fight my desire for him, and lose shamefully. Arousal leaks down my thighs as he holds me against the edge of the counter, against the edge of orgasm, and strikes my ass again and again.

My husky cry is cut off with his hand over my mouth, then his lips as he kisses me into a boneless puddle. With his body bowed over my back and his fingers in my pussy, he grips his cock and rubs the broad head across my backside, down my hip, and slides it between my legs. It's so hot and hard it feels like a fire iron driving through my folds.

I want it. I fucking need it rough and deep and right now, but I manage to gather enough brain cells to say, "Just the tip."

With a harsh laugh, he fists my hair, wrenches my head to the side, and breathes heavily, fiercely, against my neck. "I'm already all in. This is just a technicality."

Then he thrusts, burying himself to the root.

I choke on a soundless scream as my body stretches around his girth. He groans deeply, gutturally, and his hands fly to my hips, yanking me tighter against him as his forehead drops to my spine.

Holy fuck, he's thick and huge and *hard*. So fucking hard I'm certain my cervix just rammed into my stomach.

"Goddamn, Laynee." He plows into me with ruthless strokes. "I feel everything. Every ridge inside you. Every tight clench. It's so good. So damn good." He stares down at where we're joined, grunting with each thrust and sighing through every exhale. "Wish you could see this. The way your cunt grips my cock. It's fucking perfect."

My nipples harden, and my lungs slam together. I feel him throbbing inside me, swelling and lengthening as I clamp down around him. His groans are like a drug. The tremors in his hands are the elixir. He's affected by this, by *me*, and his intoxicating responses feed my addiction.

He kicks my feet apart, adjusting my body the way he wants it, and drives his hips into a frantic rhythm. "Look at me."

The moment I meet his eyes in the mirror, I know

I've lost. His expression is so full of passion and devotion as he watches my reflection. My stupid heart pounds in my throat, fully engaged and begging for forever.

Don't hurt me.

He tangles his fingers in my hair and brings his mouth to the corner of mine.

Don't leave me.

He kisses a trail along my jaw that ends at my ear with his breaths caressing my neck. He never breaks eye contact, never slows the pace of his thrusts. The connection, the fusion of our bodies, the grip on my hair, and the intimacy of his eyes—all of it shoves me over the ledge.

I come apart around him, grinding and moaning and clawing at the counter. He rocks me through it, rolling his hips and cradling my head, with his parted lips pressed against my jaw.

"That was beautiful." He kicks his hips, tormenting my overstimulated pussy. "So fucking perfect."

When he pulls out, his fingers move over my dress, searching the seams. "Where's the zipper?"

"I'll get it." I slide it down my side, twitching all over from the orgasm.

He toes off his Converse and removes his jeans and briefs. Then he grips the dress and yanks it over my head. The bra goes next, leaving me completely nude with my back to him.

He spends an anguishing amount of time kissing and stroking my scarred skin before turning me to face him. He gives my breasts and mouth the same treatment, sucking and licking with patience and adoration. Every touch of his lips and feverish caress of his hands fans my arousal, spreading it outward and reheating my body for another round.

"Are you this attentive with all women?" My whisper is breathy and cautious against his mouth.

"If you're thinking about other women, I'm not doing something right." He bites my bottom lip and clutches my shoulders, pressing them downward.

I give beneath his hands and lower to my knees. At this level, there's so much naked Decker to take in. The tension in his thighs. The heavy sac hanging beneath his long wet cock. The tight packs of his abs that ripple into chiseled pecs and broad shoulders.

He curls his fingers around his cock, angling it skyward. It's monstrous and veiny and so damn long that even with his fist at the base, there's at least five exposed inches to suck.

With slow, measured strokes, he slides his hand up and down his length so close to my face I can smell the sweet essence of our combined arousal. His other hand captures my hair, forcing my head back to gaze up at him.

He moves his fingers from my hair to cup my jaw, staring into my eyes, slowly stroking his erection, and making me crazy with need.

Several seconds pass before his knuckles slide beneath my chin. He tilts my head farther back, and his thumb draws a path from the curve of my upper lip, down to my lower lip and pressing inward, causing it to pout out.

"Open your mouth," he whispers.

My lips separate, and my pussy clenches.

"Wider." His breathing speeds up. "Yes. Just like that."

He steps closer and brushes the head of his cock

against my tongue, teasing, groaning, driving us both into a tightly-coiled fog of hunger.

"Decker." I choke on a thick swallow and grip the hard planks of his ass.

"Take it." He pushes the crown past my lips and hisses. "Fuck."

I flatten my tongue and stretch my jaw to accommodate him as he sinks another inch. And another. There's no way I can swallow his entire length.

"Such a good girl," he whispers, slowly feeding me half his hardness before pulling out and starting again.

I hold my mouth open, clutch his ass, and absorb his shallow thrusts.

The air has been knocked from my lungs, and a million doubts race through my head. I should've kicked him out the moment he disregarded my limits and spanked me. I should be on the phone with Infidelity right now, reporting his violation. It worries me that I've done nothing to defend myself. It *terrifies* me. I don't know him, yet here I am, hungrily sucking his cock.

I told this man my secrets and broke my own rules by letting him fuck me without Reese. I'm repeating mistakes, restarting the ugly cycle of terrible decisions, and I can't bring myself to stop it.

Because I'm already attached.

It could be worse. He isn't burying himself in the back of my throat or slamming against my face to get himself off. But his restraint is tenuous. I see it in the trembling of his legs, the rapid rise and fall of his chest, and the strained look on his face. He wants to unleash the animal pacing behind his eyes.

"Suck it. Don't stop." A desperate growling noise

comes from his throat. He's so vocal and worked up, humming long groans beneath his breath and whispering so softly I can't make out all the words. "Yes…good…oh, fuck…"

He slips his shaft from my mouth and yanks me off the floor. In the next breath, he crushes me against the nearest wall, with my legs around his hips and his cock buried in one hard drive.

I arch into his thrusts and hug the strong column of his neck, moaning and grinding my way toward another release.

"Fuck, Laynee." Without breaking eye contact, he lets go of his control, slamming his hips and banging me ruthlessly, wildly, against the sheetrock. "What are you doing to me?"

Gripping the back of my neck, he pulls me close and takes my mouth in a hot wet kiss. His other arm hooks around my back, working me up and down his cock. He tastes like recklessness, smells like leather and testosterone, and feels like a whipping storm of passion. I've never been with a man so emotionally and vehemently expressive with his body.

I've never felt this connected to another person.

He grabs a handful of my ass and bends forward, deepening his angle. "Give me your eyes."

I don't just give him my eyes. I give myself over to him completely. With a free-falling scream of surrender, I come on his cock with all the poise of a deliriously satisfied woman. My entire body shudders, my chest heaves for air, and my fingernails claw at his back.

He holds my gaze and pumps himself in and out erratically, panting, muscles flexing and shaking. His mouth opens. His pupils dilate, and he roars his release with a guttural, sexy-as-hell groan. It's a beautiful sight—the tendons in his neck stretched taut, lips swollen, and eyes molten and fixed on mine.

"Decker." I slump against his chest and slide my cheek along the sharp angles of his. "I love watching you come."

He trembles and twitches against me, the hardened flesh of his chest feverish and damp. "It's never been that good. Ever."

Pinning me to the wall with his body, he doesn't pull out as he cradles my face in his hands and kisses me languorously, breathlessly, and with more affection than I know what to do with.

It's too late to hold on to the vulnerable pieces of myself. He's already taken them, and in exchange, he's given me hope. Hope that he won't hurt me. Hope that this will last.

Hope is the most dangerous incentive of all.

Chapter 19

Decker

The next four months are as intense and hungry as that afternoon in the L.A. dressing room. It's strange how I don't miss being single and unattached. I sure as hell don't miss the loneliness of my studio apartment. In fact, I've discovered a fuckton of perks in living with a woman.

One woman in particular.

When I wake morning or night, I only have to reach over to fill my hands with a perfect set of tits. When I'm in a bad mood or not feeling well, she's at my side, soothing me with affection and concern—something I don't remember ever receiving, not even from my mother. It also feels fucking amazing to be instructing again. She's just one student, but watching her flex her new-found confidence on the wrestling mats has renewed my passion in teaching. When she kicks my ass, the sound of her laughter is intoxicating. It's made me greedy for more.

Getting to know her has given me a glimpse of what it might be like to share a life with someone. *With her.* The simplest things—preparing her meals, leaving her admiring notes, finding ways to show her how much she means to me, making her happy—has altered my definition of *getting ahead.*

Infidelity pulled me out of a rut, but it's become

clear to me that success isn't measured in dollar signs or notches in a bedpost. Over the past few months, I've counted my greatest accomplishments in the number of times I put a smile on Laynee's face.

I don't know when it happened, but at some point, she's become my purpose. Her happiness is my incentive. She's my secret to getting ahead in life.

With long vigorous strokes, I slice through the water in the pool behind her Georgian-style cottage. Each time I come up for air, my gaze falls unerringly on her toned, lithe body on the lounger.

Face down with her feet angled toward me, she offers up a sinful view of her delectable ass. Little black strings crisscross her curves and hold the tiny pieces of her bikini together. I don't know why she bothers wearing anything at all. It's a Friday night. No one's around. She's going to be nude as soon as I finish my laps in the pool.

Christ, I love the way she bends to my touch, melts beneath my mouth, and unravels around my cock. I have her—beside me, under me, all around me—yet I feel like I'm still chasing her.

The golden waves of her hair part down her back and fall around her ribs, baring a tapestry of scars that shimmer like diamonds in the glow of dusk. In the five months I've known her, she's never exposed them to anyone but me. Reese was there the night she was attacked, but if he showed up right now, she'd wrap a towel around her shoulders.

It bugs me. Not that I want her parading around half-nude in front of other people. But I don't like her hiding in shame. In fact, it fucking pisses me off.

Her fans idolize her, and her public image is recovering with the buzz about her dating a handsome nobody. Not because that nobody is me, but because she's making public appearances again, putting herself out there. Except the world has no idea what she's concealing beneath her designer clothes.

I've been dragging her out of the house a couple times a week. I take her to dinner, dancing in night clubs, sunbathing on the beaches of Tybee Island. We've also made several day trips to L.A. for various interviews and meetings. The cameras follow her everywhere, and I despise the smile she gives them, the one that doesn't reach her gorgeous blue eyes.

There's something standing in the way of her happiness, something big and jagged inside her that projects a shadowy wall behind her gaze. I know what it is. I have a despicably close relationship with it.

Because I saw it in the eyes of a nine-year-old boy.

I watched it permanently steal his smile.

I felt it when his mother pulled him out of my school.

Broken trust.

It's a crippling scar on the soul.

I'm not guilty of the horrors that were done to those kids. Nor am I guilty of the abuse that was inflicted on Laynee.

But I want to be guilty of repairing the damage. Even if it takes forever. Hell, I'll give her infinite forevers to see her whole and happy.

The problem is I don't know my way around a relationship. My experience with women is limited to sex. When I want it, I chase it—through seduction, domination, whatever means necessary. But the best sex in the world won't rebuild Laynee's eroded trust.

Even though I have her, she remains out of reach,

aloof, *sad.* All of this became apparent to me when she wasn't offered the role in her last audition. It was given to an actress with half her talent and beauty. The actress also happens to be half her age, which was a devastating blow to Laynee's morale.

Adding insult to injury, I came home from that trip with business cards from two potential investors. Both divorced women, loaded with capital and looking for ways to invest it. Given the way they leered at me, they're probably more interested in my cock than my business ideas, so I don't know if anything will come from the proposals I sent them.

The prospect of me working with them hasn't helped the ominous mood hanging over Laynee. Especially since she offered numerous times to fund my business ventures. Taking money from the woman I want to provide for feels like a kick to the groin. I need to do this on my own.

"Earth to Decker."

Her lilt draws my gaze to her hypnotic eyes.

"What's putting that sexy brooding look on your face?" She shifts to sit on the end of the lounger and stretches out her bare legs in the space between us.

Standing in the shallow end, I rest my forearms on the concrete ledge and curl my hands around her delicate ankles. "Where do you see us at the end of this agreement?"

"Oh. I…" Her spine straightens, and she glances away. "It's too soon to—"

"We're almost halfway through the year. Tell me what you want, Laynee."

"I'd rather not," she whispers.

"Too bad." I tighten my grip on her legs. "Tell me anyway."

Her lips sink into a frown, and she makes a grumbling sound in her throat. "I want you to stay." Her eyes bounce to mine. "But I'll ruin it. I'll ruin whatever we create because I always do. I suck at relationships."

"Bullshit. You've maintained a relationship with Reese for ten years."

"We're not fucking."

And they never will, if Reese wants to keep breathing.

"Your friendship with him proves you know how to get close to someone, how to take a leap of trust." I run my palms up and down her calves, marveling at the illumination of her eyes in the lingering light of the sunset. "Did you know that up until a couple months ago, I had no friendships to speak of."

"That's not true." Her nose scrunches. "What about that Dan guy you gave your apartment to?"

"I kept him at a distance when I lived in New York. It wasn't until I met you that I started talking to him on the phone all the time. Then there's my other unlikely friends."

"Reese." She smiles.

I smile with her because my friendship with him makes her ridiculously happy. If I'm honest, I actually enjoy hanging out with the posh bastard. So much so I've turned our guys' night out into a weekly thing.

"And my sponsor," I say.

Much to my surprise, I've kept in contact with Dr. Evan Daniels. I call him more than I care to admit and even met him for drinks when he was in Savannah for a conference last month. Of course, she doesn't know his identity. He knows her, only because he's seen me photographed with her.

"What's your point?" she asks.

"After what went down with my best friend and business partner, I cut everyone out of my life. I didn't think I'd ever be able to let someone in again. You showed me how."

"I didn't—"

"You trusted me with your secrets, Laynee. That took guts." My gaze roams over her lickable body, and I slide her a smile that says I love what I see. "I figured if this tiny wisp of a woman had the balls to expose her fears to me, I could man up and let a few people into my personal life."

"Man up?" She glances at my torso, my arms, and lingers on my lips. Her nipples tighten beneath the bikini. "If anything, you need to man *down*. Wouldn't want you to get testosterone poisoning."

"That's not a thing." My cock twitches in my swim trunks.

"You're wrong." Her lips purse, and she leaps to her feet, breaking my hold on her ankles. "It's a known ailment." She backs up with a flicker of heat dancing in her eyes. "It usually manifests at puberty and results in behavior that defies common sense."

I lean into my arms and lift out of the pool, splattering the concrete with a deluge of water from my shorts as I stalk toward her. "What kind of behavior?"

"Well…" Backstepping toward the house, she loses a fight with her smile. "Typical dumb male behavior, like strutting and flexing and…gun cocking."

I follow her gaze to the stiffy straining my wet shorts and drop my voice a few octaves. "You should probably run."

With a sharp inhale, she spins and darts into the house. My pulse spikes as I chase her heart-shaped ass through the kitchen and past the hearth room before catching her in the living room. I'm soaking wet, and my feet slip across the tiles, so it's an ungraceful impact of drenched skin and heavy breaths when I slam into her.

I brace for a tumble, maybe even a half-hearted struggle. What I don't expect is the punch she sends toward my head. I dodge it, anticipating a follow through like I taught her. Adrenaline floods my veins as her second swing forces my body backwards.

She misses. I grin. She grins back and rears her arm for a third strike. I'm ready.

Her knee connects with my groin. She doesn't just crunch my erection. She attacks from underneath, striking in an upward motion and splitting the tri-state region with the maximum amount of pain.

"Fuuuuck!" I bend at the waist, sucking air, my muscles momentarily inhibited because she invoked my damn spinal reflex.

Holy fucking shit, that hurts.

"Oh my God." She hugs my bowed head to her chest and strokes my hair. "I'm so sorry. I didn't mean to—"

I sweep her feet out from beneath her, brace her fall on the floor, and land atop her. "You should've kept running."

"I can't." She cups my face and stares into my eyes, gasping from exertion. "Don't you get it?"

"Then why am I still chasing you?"

"Because you have an old lady fetish."

I grip her neck and apply enough pressure to get her attention. "Age is a shallow measurement. Think deeper, Laynee."

"You say deeper, and my mind turns into a

gutter." She pulls at my fingers on her throat. "How's your balls?"

"Throbbing." I trail my hand from her neck, over her breast, and drag down the bikini top, exposing her fleshy tit. "That maneuver was really badass, baby. Major turn on."

She laughs, eyes sparkling in the lamp light. "Only you can take a shot below the belt and maintain an erection."

"Only you can give me an erection."

"You're so full of shit."

With a hard pinch, I tweak her nipple and continue downward, following the curve of her waist, her hip, and her flat stomach, before sinking my fingers beneath the scrap of her swimsuit bottoms. The material is cold and wet from my dripping shorts, and goosebumps pebble her flesh. She's shivering, and not in a good way.

In a blur of movement, I strip us both out of the wet clothes and carry her to the couch. Reclining on my back, I spread her nude body over the length of mine and rub my hands over her back and thighs, warming her satiny skin.

She feels like heaven in my arms. Every caress fuels my desire for her. Pulsing heat surges through my cock, making me harder, hungrier. Her breathing increases, quickening my own breaths. I can't stop myself from gripping the base of my cock and guiding it toward her soft hot center. I desperately need to be inside her. But in the back of my mind, there's a conversation on pause. A necessary conversation.

"Tell me why I feel like I'm still chasing you." I roll my hips beneath her, gliding the tip along her folds while plunging my fingers into her wet heat and teasing us both.

She swallows a moan and braces her hands on the cushion above my head. "We're together…"

"But?"

Christ, she's soaked. Throbbing around my fingers. So fucking ready to take my cock.

"This isn't togetherness." She lowers her forehead to mine. "Sex isn't love, Decker. Not for men like you."

I groan. "Men like me?"

Fuck, I try to make sense of her words, but my brain is operating on a single circuit. *Hot naked woman. Wet pussy. Must thrust.*

"Yes, men like you." She pulls my hand out from between us and takes over, curling her fingers around me and adjusting the angle. "Men who can do this and walk away without giving the woman another thought."

She lowers herself on my cock, and the tight clasp of her body sucks me in and zaps my ability to think.

"Ahhhh, fuck." My muscles spasm against an onslaught of pleasure. "Fucking love your cunt, Laynee. Give me your mouth." I reach for her neck to yank her closer.

She knocks my hand away. "We're still talking."

Why I thought I could hold a conversation while buried inside her is beyond me. All I want to do is flip her over and pound her into multiple orgasms.

After a few calming breaths, I remind myself I initiated this heart-to-heart. Because it's important. Much more important than the unholy ache gathering in my balls.

"You're crazy if you think I can walk away from this and never think of you again." I brush a thumb across her pouty lips. "I'm not sure I can walk away from you at all."

"Why not?" She squints at me suspiciously and lowers her chest to mine, inadvertently rubbing her nipples against my skin. It's fucking distracting.

"I'm really struggling to put two words together here." My chuckle comes out as a pained groan.

"Try." She grips my jaw, her expression intense. "Why don't you think you can walk away?"

"Because this is different." I hold her stare. "I know that sounds like a banal platitude, but it's the truth. *You* are different."

Her pussy clamps down on me, wrenching a guttural sound from my throat and begging me to thrust.

"Don't do that." I grab her ass and give her a hard warning squeeze. "No clenching."

She laces her fingers together on my chest and props her chin on her hands, putting her sweet little mouth a kiss away. "Why is this different?"

"You're killing me." I lick my lips. "I've never had a conversation during sex. Nor have I ever fucked the same woman more than a couple times."

Her expression darkens, and I realize that was the absolute wrong thing to say.

I cup the side of her face. "I've never cared about someone enough to commit to a relationship."

"You committed to an agreement, Decker. One that gives you a monthly salary. And sex every day. And investors for your business venture."

My jaw stiffens. "I hate that goddamn agreement because it makes you doubt what's going on here. But I don't regret signing it because it brought us together." I push my fingers through her hair and try to ignore the torment of her pussy pulsing around my cock. "As for the investors, I'm not a leech. I *need* financial independence."

"See? That's exactly what—"

I cover her mouth with my hand. "I don't want income so I can leave you." I stroke her lips and move my hand to her hair. "I'm a proud man, Laynee. I can't sit here on my ass and live off your money. That's not the way I'm built. I need to feel like I'm contributing. I need to know I can support you and protect you in every way."

Her eyes soften, and she melts against me with a heavy sigh. "You still haven't said why. Why me?"

"If you want me to wax poetic, you got the wrong guy. My feelings are simple. My stomach hurts when I think about sleeping without you. I get moody and sulky when you lock yourself in your office. I hate when I don't have access to you. Because I fucking love to look at you. I even enjoy listening to you ramble on about shit. You don't bore me. In fact, I can't think of a single second I've been bored in the past five months. That's pretty fucking novel for a *man like me*. And right now, your tight cunt is squeezing the fuck out of my dick, and there isn't another goddamn place I'd rather be."

"That's…" Her lashes drift downward, shielding her eyes. "That's a better answer than I expected."

She rewards me by shifting her hips and slowly riding my cock. I let her rock and grind until my need to devour her shreds my self-control. Flipping her onto her back, I give her my dick the way we both need it—hard, uncivilized, and full of fire.

Her throaty moans tighten my balls. I capture her mouth and kiss her with the same urgency and vigor as the hammer of my hips. I feed on her sexy sounds and roll with the undulation of her killer body. When the coiling impulse to come grips the base of my spine, I fight it back. I'm not ready for this to end. I'll never be done with this woman.

Sex isn't love. Not for men like you.

She's wrong. I've fucked so many women, too many, and it's never felt like this. It was always about chasing the release and getting the hell out of Dodge. But with Laynee, I want to stay right here, inside her, with her. Forget the orgasm. Every thrust into her body is an expression of deep, strong, possessive, mind-over-body insanity. If that isn't love, then the damn concept doesn't exist.

"I don't want to come." I drive into her, pressing against the back of her pussy, aching for her to feel me the way I feel her.

"You have to, Decker." She bites at my lips then kisses me deeply, passionately, the only way she knows how. "I'll take it personally if you don't."

I wrap her legs around my waist and savor her whimpers and husky little breaths as she digs her heels into my ass.

"We'll do it together." I lift her chin, forcing her gaze to mine.

She nods, swallows. "I'm close."

"You're going to look at me when you come."

"Okay." Her forehead pinches in concentration, and her tits bounce against my chest, teasing and tormenting.

"You have such a great rack."

"You talk too much." Her pinched lips slip beneath a grin before flattening again.

"I want to know—"

"Shut it." She closes her eyes.

"What goes on in that sexy head when you're trying to come?"

She sighs. Then her eyes focus on mine, and her pupils are so big they swallow the blue. "I think about how huge and hard your cock is and how lucky I am to have it ramming inside me." She gasps on the next thrust and fists her hands in my hair. "I think about how the thundering sound of your heart means you're into this. Into *me*. I imagine you being so desperate for me that you'd punch anyone who tries to come between us and this amazing feeling. You'd battle an army of Gladiators, fight off a pack of wolves—"

"Gladiators and wolves?"

"Shh. This is my fantasy." She tightens the muscles in her pussy, making my eyes roll back in my head. "You'd snarl and growl and bare your fangs, marking your territory, protecting me from danger, all while finding pleasure in my body. And you keep coming back for more. Because this means something to you. And maybe, just maybe you'll…" Her lashes lower. "Stay."

Christ, this woman. I grab the back of her head and kiss her until there's no oxygen left in the room. Until the crescendo of her moans rise in volume and intensity, and her body trembles on the peak of release.

"This means everything to me." I kiss her again then pull her head back to stare into her eyes and watch her explode. I fall with her, instantly, violently, shooting my load and roaring to the ceiling. The force of it stops my heart and stuns me into a breathless stupor. It takes me several minutes to gather my bearings. I have just enough energy left to roll us on the couch so that she's on top and not crushed by my weight.

"I think I just died." I close my eyes with a stupid

smile on my face.

"Hmm." The evil hussy slides up and down on my cock, laughing. "You're dead and still hard? Why am I not surprised?"

I pull her against me and bury my face in her neck. "You smell like the sweetest incentive."

"Incentive?"

"Incentive to die with you in my arms."

She releases a soft sated breath and goes limp against me, twining our legs and tangling her fingers in my hair. I'm overcome with the need to hold her closer, to watch over her and guard her from anything or anyone who might cause her harm. It makes me feel vulnerable and…scared. Through utter ignorance, I failed in protecting the students in my school. What if I fail her, too?

The rapid rhythm of our breaths eases into contented silence. She lies so still and lethargic on top of me, I wonder if she's awake. Long moments pass before her fingers twitch and lift to trace the line of my jaw.

"I've been doing a lot of thinking." She skims her hand down my throat and flattens her palm over my heart. "About my past relationships. And my current one."

"I'm listening." I pull the blanket off the back of the couch, wrap it around us, and press my lips against her head.

She snuggles closer against my neck. "My experience with the people I'm closest to has made me question what it means to be intimate. And to be in love. I blame myself for the neglect, the betrayal, and abuse—"

"That's unacceptable. You're not—"

"I'm not defending their actions. Let me finish."

She flexes and loosens her hand on my chest. "My parents loved me, but they never gave up anything for that love. I thought I loved Trey and Blake and even Reese…"

I tense beneath her. "Reese?"

"I do love him, Decker. As a friend. I never definitively understood why he and I couldn't be more than friends until you enlightened me about his submissive nature. We could've worked through that, but we didn't. We didn't even try. He would've never given up his need to…"

"Be fucked in the ass?"

"We really need to work on your refinement." She laughs. "But yes, his need to be a bottom, and I was unwilling to understand his needs. None of my relationships have followed the law of sacrifice, and that's where I screwed up. I've been so consumed by the idea of someone loving me that I was willing to settle on any one who flashed me a doting smile. I overlooked flaws, shady behavior, adultery…terrible things. What I should've done all along was look internally. I should've asked myself, *What will you give up for this man?* Had I done that with Trey or Blake, the answer would've been *Nothing*. I wouldn't have sacrificed a thing for them because deep down, I knew they were wrong for me."

One could argue she sacrificed the flawless skin on her back for the son of a bitch who stabbed her, but that's not what she means. She didn't willingly let him hurt her.

The self-centered part of me is more focused on how this conversation applies to her and me. I know she's asking herself what she'd give up for me. And it goes both ways. Does she want me to walk away from my pursuit to start up a new school? Something else?

"You're quiet," she whispers against my neck.

"What do you mean by the law of sacrifice?"

"The best way to gauge how much you love someone is by how much you're willing to sacrifice for them. I'm not talking about dramatic gestures, like giving up your career or taking a bullet. It's the little things, forfeiting tiny parts of yourself that have lesser value than the thing you're trying to attain."

"What are you trying to attain?"

"Love." She lifts her head, peering up at me. "Am I freaking you out?"

"A little. Only because I'm a guy, and you're speaking a language I've never understood."

She moves to lie on the center of my body, chest to chest with her elbows propped on my shoulders. "I want you to stay. Not because we renewed the agreement. Not because you need income and investors and a celebrity girlfriend. I want you to stay for the right reasons, and I don't want to fuck this up. I've never been willing to fully surrender myself to anyone, but when I'm with you, I want to relinquish my fears, my defenses, my rules and hard limits out of devotion. *And trust.* I want you to stay because *your* heart is enriched by sacrifice."

Her words fill me with a feeling of breathlessness that radiates through my chest. "What have I sacrificed?"

"You could've kept the money you made in your business, could've reinvested it in another venture." She searches my face, her eyes bright and clear. "You gave up your livelihood for those kids. You gave up everything. And that makes me want to be a better person. I want to make sacrifices. For you."

Through all this talk about sacrifice, she hasn't once asked me to give up a damn thing for her. It dawns on me with frightening clarity that I would forfeit, forgo, and surrender anything and everything for her.

I shift us into a sitting position, arranging her legs around my waist and hugging her chest to mine. "Before you start making offerings to me like I'm some kind of sex god, because…well, we both know I've earned that status…"

"Oh, brother." She rolls her eyes, grinning.

I smile with her, kiss her lips, and let the humor drain from my face. "You're going to make a sacrifice for someone else."

Her gorgeous face creases in confusion. "Who?"

"You, Laynee."

"I don't understand."

I lift her off my lap, clasp her hand, and lead her upstairs to the bedroom. A few weeks ago, I did something rash and irreversible, something that will make my petite beauty seethe with murderous wrath when she finds out. Knowing the outcome won't be pleasant, I took the fearless-man route and put off telling her.

Every year, she hosts a charity event for battered women. It's one of those exclusive dinner-for-a-cause affairs, where glamorous people pay fifty grand a plate to rub elbows, flash their fancy clothes, and bid on sports memorabilia, famous gowns and jewelry, and elite services. Held in Savannah, the event brings in hundreds of celebrities, paparazzi, and massive media coverage, all of which results in millions of dollars for victims of abuse.

The event is tomorrow night.

I release her hand in the bedroom and pull on a pair of workout shorts. She doesn't know it yet, but we're on the cusp of a raging argument. I won't go into it with my junk hanging out like a target.

She follows my lead and puts on one of my t-shirts, watching me with tapered eyes. "What are you up to, Decker Gabrielli?"

I step into the closet and return with a garment bag. A couple months ago, the famous designer, Victoria Beckham, created a floor-length gown for Laynee, specifically for tomorrow night's charity dinner. Laynee didn't notice it missing from the closet the past couple weeks.

"What are you doing with that?" Her eyebrows pull together.

"Open it." I lay it on the bed and step back, my pulse pounding in my throat.

She unzips the bag, and her hands slide over the black satin. I'm not a fashion guru, but the high neck and plain sheath style seemed rather drab and boring. But that's not why I had it altered.

It cost me thousands of dollars at the best dress shop in Savannah. I've since learned that the price I paid for alterations was a small fraction of what the gown is worth.

She casts me a perplexed look and lifts the dress from the bag. I hold my breath.

As she turns it over to inspect the back, the blood drains from her face.

"What the—?" Her hands tremble, searching the seams. "No." She gasps, whispers. "*NoNoNoNoNo.*" Chest heaving, she tosses the material on the bed and glares at it with horrified shock. "Where the fuck is the back of the dress?"

"It's been sacrificed." I step into her space, cradle her face in my hands, and hold her gaze with mine. "Sacrificed for something greater. Something *extraordinary.*"

Nothing is more extraordinary than her strength and survival. It's time for her to wear her scars with pride, and there isn't a better way for her to expose them than at a charity for abused women.

Her show of bravery will inspire her celebrity friends to donate more money to the cause. The media will celebrate her acceptance of her imperfections, and amid the overwhelming support, Laynee will finally heal.

I don't realize until later how very wrong I am—about all of it.

CHAPTER 20

Laynee

Oh God, this can't be happening. I jerk away from Decker's touch and pace the bedroom. A feverish chill engulfs my body, and a lump the size of Georgia lodges in my throat.

"You destroyed my fucking gown." I can't believe it. I'm staring at the backless sheath of satin, and it still doesn't seem real. "Ninety thousand dollars, Decker. I paid *ninety* thousand dollars for that dress."

"Try it on." He cocks his head, his voice infuriatingly calm. *He doesn't get it.*

"Fuck you." I storm toward him, pointing a shaky finger at the bed. "You fucking ruined it!"

"Your reaction has nothing to do with the damn dress and everything to do with fear."

Fear? I know fear. I've been carrying it around for six years. Fear that a director will demand I do a scene with my back exposed. Fear that I'll have a wardrobe malfunction in public, and one of my scars will show through. Fear that my imperfections will be leaked to the media, and the hateful world will body-shame me into an early grave.

This isn't fear. It's raw scorching anger, burning through my veins and depriving my lungs of air. My ears ring. My stomach coils, and tears saturate my eyes.

I can't stand among my judgmental peers and

flashing cameras with my back disfigured. I live in a world of superficial expectations, where celebrities don't have wrinkles or belly fat or scars. The smallest imperfection is lambasted. I would no longer be seen as Laynee Somerset, a regal class act. I would be known as the poor, beaten-down has-been.

Blinking away my tears, I look him in the eyes. "What story do you propose I tell the press? That I let my stalker move in with me, and when he stabbed me in the back, I had him killed?"

He sits beside the dress on the edge of the bed and rests his elbows on his knees. "You were attacked. Bludgeoned within an inch of your life. But you *survived*. That's all you tell them. Let them investigate and dig. They won't find anything, right?"

"No," I say quietly. "They won't find anything at all."

Only Decker, Reese, and the surgeon know about the scars. Elijah, my head of security, is the man who arranged Trey's car accident. He knows something happened, but he never demanded details. I trust him with my life.

But that's beside the point. Decker made a crucial decision without me, one that impacts my life.

"You had no right." I drag a hand through my hair, my entire body shaking with betrayal, hurt, and fury.

What am I going to do? I have dozens of designer gowns in my closet, but I've been photographed in all of them. Donning an already-worn dress would result in speculation about my finances. *Has Laynee Somerset run out of money? Has she burned out her career? No wonder she moved back to Savannah.*

It's all bullshit, but this is my life. If my fans don't

believe in me, producers won't even look at me. My career will be over.

Anger boils anew, vibrating through my voice. "I'm so fucking pissed off at you right now I can't see straight."

"I expected that."

"Then why'd you do it?"

The arrogant bastard lifts a brow as if the question is unreasonable.

I know he's thinking about the conversation we just had downstairs, but he altered my dress long before that. "You weren't thinking about sacrifice when you made this decision for me."

"No." Head down, he locks his hands together between his spread legs and watches from beneath dark brows. "I was thinking about how beautiful your body is. Every exquisite inch of skin. I was thinking about how inspiring it will be to other abuse victims when they see Laynee Somerset hold her head high and wear her skin with dignity."

He stands from the bed, crosses the room, and disappears in the closet, leaving me alone with a bubbling cauldron of emotions. His intent is honest, but he doesn't fully grasp the ramifications. I wish I could ignore the ridicule and hatred, but I don't have that luxury. I love my career, and I've worked too damn hard to lose it all over a show of courage.

I lift the dress and hold it up to inspect the back. The satin cuts low, and the front wraps around to tie at the neck. If I'm honest, the style is sexier, more eye-catching than the original. I used to prefer backless gowns, used to love to show off the curve of my spine. But that was before.

Footsteps approach, and he steps around me,

holding a bundle of silver fur. Some kind of shawl?

"The lady at the shop called this a capelet." He wraps it around my shoulders and catches the drape in the back, pressing it against my tailbone. "It covers your entire back."

I set down the gown, and a flutter takes flight in my chest as I run my fingers over the luxurious pelt of the shawl. "Is it real?"

"Faux fur." He slides his hands over my shoulders, lowering the wrap to hang around my upper arms. "It's handmade per my specifications."

With a shuddering breath, I step to the full-length mirror in the corner and finger the scarf-like drape of fur around my chest. Hidden hooks clasp the ends together, allowing a snug fit that won't slide or slip.

It's a beautiful accent piece and appropriate for the season. Winter evenings in Savannah are chilly. It shows off my shoulders and will give the black satin gown a classy unique look.

"I didn't make the decision for you, Laynee." He stands behind me and touches his lips to my neck. "I merely packaged the choice in satin, tied it with a fur bow, and gave it to you to open."

"I'm not opening it." I meet his eyes in the mirror. "I can't. You know that, right?"

Frustration darkens his features.

"Don't give me that look." I return my attention to my reflection and cringe at the teary pink skin around my eyes. "You think I'm a coward."

"If I thought you were a coward, I wouldn't have bothered with the dress." He grips my waist from behind and rests his cheek against mine, taking in the view of us in the mirror. "You don't believe this, but I already know you're going to walk out of that event with your shoulders back, chin high, and the elegant lines of your back on full display. And I'm going to be the lovesick asshole standing at your side."

Is he saying he loves me? An excruciating burn swallows my chest and pricks my eyes. "I want that. I do. But I'm scared."

"I know, baby, but you'll do it anyway." His arms encircle my waist and pull my back flush with his chest. "You're going to look fear in the face and make it your bitch."

CHAPTER 21

Laynee

The next night, I exit the bedroom and walk down the stairs in sky-high stilettos, following the deep rumble of Decker's voice. My nerves are through the roof as I curl my fingers in the silver fur around my arms and curse it for the hundredth time.

He might not have made the decision for me, but in his usual controlling, arm-twisting fashion, he's made it painfully hard to not consider his demand. If I remove the shawl, I risk a damaging blow to my public image. If I keep it on, I face his disappointment. The former shrivels my insides, but the latter is more than I can bear.

As I reach the bottom step, I spot him near the front door immersed in conversation with Reese. Since Decker got ready for the charity ball in the guest bedroom, we haven't seen each other yet. They don't notice me standing around the corner, so I take a minute to appreciate the view.

Fingers tucked in their front pockets and postures relaxed but strong, they wear black tuxedos and easy smiles. Decker's at least an inch taller, and his chest and shoulders are broader. Reese's perfectly-plastered hair looks blonder than normal beside Decker's brown finger-raked mess of sexiness.

Sweet hell, they're gorgeous beyond words, but

Decker's the one who steals my focus and quickens my breaths. Flawlessly tailored black pants stretch enticingly across his groin, and the crisp white collar shirt deepens the glow of his tan complexion. Plump lips crook with cocky arrogance, and dark brows maintain that roguish look I love so much.

His eyes lift, and I'm consumed by the intensity that dominates his expression. Affection, desire, wicked intent—it's all there as he peruses me from tits to toes and back again before landing on my face.

"Fuck, Laynee." Hooking a finger beneath his collar, he tugs at the silver bow tie and goes back for another full-body scan that makes me feel naked and overdressed at the same time. But more than that, he makes me feel beautiful.

"You look like…" He wets his lips. "A movie star."

"She *is* a movie star, asshat." Reese squints at him. "You can do better than that."

"I know." Decker rubs the back of his neck, his attention glued to the vicinity of my satin-covered crotch. "I'm thinking with the wrong head at the moment."

The iridescence of his golden-brown eyes and the sultry smile occupying his lips burns me up from the inside out. I step toward him, devouring the trim fit of his tux, the day-old stubble he rebelliously left on his face, and the taunting way his straight white teeth sink into the corner of his bottom lip.

When I reach him, he curls strong fingers around my hips beneath the fur, stroking his thumbs against my abs. "You're exceptionally beautiful. Sinful. Peerless." He leans in, brushing his mouth along my jaw. "And mine."

His silken tone shivers through me and settles into a deep pulse between my legs.

Pulling me closer, he feathers the backs of his fingers over my breast and groans into the space beside my ear. "You're not wearing a bra."

"Didn't have a choice." *Someone sacrificed the back out of my dress.*

"Gorgeous as always, Laynee," Reese says. "I'll be waiting in the limo." He looks at Decker. "Try not to do any more damage to her gown."

The front door closes behind him, leaving me alone with Decker and his spicy masculine scent.

"You told him?" My breath hitches at the electric caress of his lips on my neck.

"I mentioned it while we were waiting." He fingers a blonde ringlet dangling from the complicated twist of my vintage-inspired updo. "Ready?"

He's not going to jump on the topic of my dress? I'm wearing the shawl with growing certainty that I won't have the courage to remove it. But if he pushes me, I might cave. Luckily, he doesn't bring it up.

He doesn't mention it during the twenty-minute ride to the Mansion on Forsyth Park. Doesn't say a thing when we exit the limo at the hotel and pose for the strobe of cameras flanking the red-carpet entrance. Without a word, he releases my arm and joins Reese near the front doors while I answer questions about the event.

My security team drove separately. They won't be entering the building, but they'll have eyes on every exit point.

Only a few selected members of the press are allowed inside. The hotel is completely sold out, every room purchased on my dime to ensure exclusivity to the attendees. No one gets into the hotel tonight without a ticket.

This is the sixth year I've hosted the charity dinner, and I hire teams of people to organize every detail of the event. I only need to show up, give an inspiring speech, and make small talk with my fellow celebrities. I usually dread these kinds of things, but this event is different. *Personal.* Leveraging my clout and money, I've made this annual gala one of the most successful fundraisers in the country.

Pulling myself away from the overzealous swarm of reporters, I try to ignore the dread twisting my insides. If Decker expected me to remove the shawl for the press, the disappointment on his face will rob me of strength.

As I glide up the stairs to the entrance, I lift my head and find the molten brown of his eyes shining with happiness and aimed straight at me. My dread vaporizes, if only for a moment. The night's just begun. If I'm going to unveil my scars, it makes sense to do it inside, safely away from the vultures. He must be thinking this, too.

It's a slow journey through the hotel as I'm stopped repeatedly by nosy actresses, who are more interested in the man on my arm than the objective of the charity. Reese wanders off, and I keep Decker moving toward the ballroom, limiting my answers with feigned amusement.

He's my boyfriend.

He doesn't model.

Yes, I know he's unbelievably handsome.

No, you cannot take him home with you.

Decker grins through all the flirting and lingering looks, his hand warm and possessive on my lower back, beneath the fur, directly against my scarred skin. As if I need a reminder of what he wants me to do tonight.

In the ballroom, gowns of every color glitter with jewels in a sea of black tuxedos. We mingle with the rich and famous, sip from champagne flutes, and make our way through the crowd.

"Miss Somerset."

I turn toward the feminine southern twang, and an authentic smile possesses my lips. "Mrs. Montague. Thank you so much for coming."

"Wouldn't miss it, dear." The older woman presses a warm kiss to my cheek and shifts her huge blue eyes to Decker. "I hoped you would introduce me to your handsome companion."

"Yes, of course." I place a hand on his muscular back. "This is Decker Gabrielli. Decker, meet Mrs. Adelaide Montague Fitzgerald."

Adelaide is one of the few in attendance who's not in the movie business. But she's an icon in her own right. The epitome of purebred Southern aristocracy, she's the tobacco heiress of Montague Corporation and inconceivably wealthy.

She's also married and a few years older than me, which is why I don't balk when Decker bows his head to her hand in a gesture I've never seen him make before.

Lifting her slender arm, he touches his lips to the bend in her wrist. "It's a pleasure to make the acquaintance of one of the most beautiful women in the room."

Oh, he's really laying on the charm, but he isn't wrong. Her brown hair coils in a perfect chignon at the base of her skull, baring a delicate unwrinkled face, and the slim fit of her sparkling gown accentuates a trim figure. Her sensual beauty exudes sophistication and grace.

"Thank you, Mr. Gabrielli." She smiles and winks at me. "He's delightful."

"He has his moments." I smile with her. When he straightens, I say, "Decker, Mrs. Montague is one of the biggest supporters of this charity."

She donates an ungodly amount of money toward the cause. In the few times I've met her, her blue eyes are always bright and alert with intelligence, but I sense something darkly familiar in the depths. She hides it well, but I know what to look for. She's concealing scars. Perhaps not as corporeal as the ones on my back, but she's harboring a deep hurt. I feel it in my bones.

"You're doing a wonderful thing here, Miss Somerset." She scans the affluent crowd around us. "The initiative to raise awareness on violence against women is needful." Her voice lowers. "More needful than most people care to admit."

"Thank you," I say, pretending not to notice the way her gaze turns inward.

She blinks, clearing her eyes and focusing on Decker. "I understand you ran a successful chain of combat sports schools."

He jerks his head back, startled. "Yes, ma'am."

Evidently, Adelaide didn't need to be introduced to Decker. Given the amount of money she's sent my way, I'm not surprised she keeps tabs on me, including the man I'm dating.

He stops a passing waiter and exchanges our empty flutes for full ones. "Mrs. Montague?" He offers her a glass of champagne.

"No, thank you." She laces her fingers together in

front of her, eyes on Decker. "Are you interested in re-opening your sports schools? Perhaps similar training but with a different purpose?"

Decker shares a look with me and arches his brow at her. "Yes."

"Very good. I have a proposal for you." She tilts her head toward the veranda. "Care to walk with me for a few minutes? I'd like to get some fresh air before dinner." She holds out her elbow.

He supports her arm with his. I might've praised him for being a proper gentleman if his gaze hadn't drifted to my chest, prompting his naughty tongue to slide over his bottom lip.

"I'll be back." He meets my eyes.

I give him an encouraging smile. *Good luck.*

As he leads Adelaide toward the veranda, I shamelessly stare at his firm tuxedo-hugged ass until a pretty starlet blocks my view.

"Laynee Somerset." She erases the distance and runs her fingers over the silver fur around my arms. "This wrap is divine. Where did you get it?"

"Thank you. Someone had it made for me."

I spend the next hour entertaining guests and working my way through the crowd. Decker returns just as the first course is being served. As he prowls toward me, the room seems to stand still. Groups of women pause in conversation to watch him pass. Everything about him is arresting, but it's his gaze that narrows the world to just him and me.

I've seen countless dark eyes in my life, but none compare to the ones watching me now. They're as potent as his touch, imposing, seductive, arousing with daunting indecency. My skin tingles and heats, and my eyelids grow heavy with every step he takes in my direction. He's so powerfully intoxicating that by the time he's within reach, I'm quivering and breathless with addictive need.

"I missed you." He rests a warm hand on my neck and guides my lips to his.

My soft moan beckons his tongue, and I don't even care if there are hundreds of powerful people watching and judging our display. My arms encircle his neck as he slides his fingers around my waist, pulling me closer. The feel of his mouth, the strength of his jaw, and the support of his embrace satisfies me on a fundamental level. This man is mine, and he tastes like forever.

Too soon, he breaks the kiss to rub his nose against mine.

I suck in a much-needed breath and rest my hands on his chest. "How was your conversation with Mrs. Montague?"

"Very nice." His lips lower to my neck, twitching with a smile. Then he scrapes his teeth across my shoulder, tickling my skin and making me squirm. "She's a lovely woman."

Our eyes meet, and his expression asks me to trust him. Whatever he discussed with Adelaide put a cautious spark of excitement in his eyes. He'll tell me when he's ready.

"Okay." I straighten his bow tie and ghost my fingers over the sharp angle of his jaw.

His neck stiffens beneath my hand. A vein bulges in his forehead, his attention zeroing in on something behind me. I turn, following his gaze, and my heart sinks to my feet, taking all my blood with it.

"What the fuck is he doing here?" Decker grips my wrist, his voice low and deadly.

Blake Harridan stalks through the ballroom with his arm around an A-list actress. The very actress who was given the leading role I recently auditioned for.

"I didn't look at the final guest list," I whisper, swallowing the knot in my throat. "He's always attended this event, but I assumed with the announcement of our divorce, he would bow out this year."

My ex-husband's thick head of black hair swivels left to right. I have an awful feeling he's searching for me, despite the buxom brunette clinging to his arm. Doesn't matter how many women are in his bed. He's always looking for a new conquest, and why not? He's classically handsome with millions of drooling female fans feeding his ego. Too bad they don't know how cruel and self-absorbed he is.

"This is a charity for abuse victims." Decker glares at Blake, who has yet to notice us on the other side of the ballroom. "His presence is fucking disgusting."

Blake never acknowledged he's an abuser. The irony of showing his face here is either lost on him or he just doesn't give a damn.

When his eyes come to a stop on mine, I flash him a sickeningly fake smile. Decker goes rigid beside me. His breathing picks up, and the hand on my arm clenches.

"You have to behave yourself, Decker." I pivot to face him, cupping his neck and drawing his gaze to mine. "Any kind of violence counteracts the purpose of this event. Please remember that."

"Laynee." His jaw sets, nostrils flaring as he briefly closes his eyes. "If he approaches you, I can't promise—"

"He won't talk to me." Last time I saw him, I threatened him with a restraining order if he comes near me again. "Pretend he's not here, okay?"

With a stiff nod, Decker leads me away from Blake and toward our table near the stage where I'll be speaking.

Dinner passes in an aromatic haze of seared chicken, bacon-wrapped asparagus, and some sort of rice. I chew it but don't taste it. I can barely maintain conversation amid the riot of my nerves. It's not the speech I'm flipping out over. It's the decision I've been putting off all night.

You're going to make a sacrifice for someone else. You, Laynee.

I rest a hand over Decker's on my lap and twine our fingers together. He glances at me with eyes of gilded brown. Eyes that caress me with the sensitivity and compassion of a man in love.

He hasn't said the words, but he goes out of his way to express my importance to him, always touching me, humming tunes to my favorite songs, and leaving me random notes, like *I love the sound of your laugh. You have a killer rack. I want you happy – and naked. You are my favorite scent. I choose you, and at the end of the agreement, I'll keep choosing you.*

I'm not big on labels, but I'm desperate to call this what it is. We're in love, fiercely, completely, in an I-don't-want-to-wake-up-beside-anyone-else-ever way. He's the one. The one who will never hurt me. The one who will protect me from anyone who threatens me.

And he wants me to reveal my scars. Because he wants me to heal.

The thing is, if I do this, I'll be doing it for him, not me.

It's the little things, forfeiting tiny parts of yourself that have lesser value than the thing you're trying to attain.

He's what I'm trying to attain, and with him, I know I'll heal. Without him, I have nothing.

When the lines of servers stream into the ballroom carrying trays of desserts, it's my cue to step behind the podium. Adjusting the fur wrap around my upper arms, I move to stand.

Midway to my full height, I hesitate, bend at the waist, and touch my forehead to his temple. "I love you."

My whisper brushes his ear before my brain catches up. Why did I just admit something so vulnerable in a crowded setting? My timing is horrible.

Flushed and uncertain, I turn toward the stage. His fingers catch mine and squeeze. I sigh at the flex of muscle in his hand. He's an incredibly strong man, and his strength is amplified in the gentle yet indomitable way he cares for me. He's my lifeline. Even if he's not standing beside me on that stage, I'll be connected to him at a depth in which I've never been connected to anyone.

Steadying my breaths, I don't glance back at him until I reach the glass podium.

CHAPTER 22

Decker sits twenty-feet away, forearms resting on the table, watching me with a complicated expression. He looks like I feel. Excited. Off-balance. Possessive. It's as if we've discovered this huge incredible thing, and it's so significant and rare that if I lose it, I fear I'll never find it again. That horrible feeling, the torment that something or someone could steal him away, sucks the air from the lungs.

Reluctantly, I break our eye contact to focus on the tablet on the glass podium. The speech I prepared fills the tablet's screen, and the words blur together as the weight of hundreds of eyes press against my skin.

You're going to look fear in the face and make it your bitch.

When I finally speak, my voice is reedy and soft. I make it through the greeting, the thank yous, and the harrowing stats about abuse victims before I decide to abandon the script.

I shut off the tablet and set it to the side. Then I raise my head and find Decker in the audience. Back straight, shoulders squared, his entire bearing is at full attention. His gaze is so formidable and confident I mirror his posture, borrow his strength, and breathe a little easier.

No matter what happens, that man holds the

banged-up pieces of my soul. He'll hold all of me if I break down. He'll catch me if I fall. And he'll demand—in his surly, bossy tone—that I stand on my own feet again. I don't have to do this alone.

"Domestic abuse can happen to anyone." I scan the shadowy silhouettes in the crowd, wondering if there's any women in the audience masking her own tragic story. "Money won't protect you. Neither will prestige and fame. Abusers prey on those who love them, and their victims never escape the effects of the violence. It follows. It haunts. It never lets go."

My fingers tremble as I touch the hooks on my shawl. "Violence comes in many forms—physical, sexual, psychological, emotional. The scars you can't see are the ones that cut the deepest, hurt the most, and take the longest to heal."

Sweat forms on my skin, and a feverish chill sweeps through me. I meet Decker's dark eyes and unclasp the hooks on the fur wrap. Holding his steady gaze, I slip the shawl off and drape it over the podium. My heart races. My knees weaken, and a surge of panic spikes through me. I glance over my shoulder and find no one behind me or in the vicinity of the stage. No one can see my disfigurement.

Releasing a ragged breath, I lean closer to the microphone. "Victims of abuse are resilient. They learn how to adapt and self-edit to prevent the abuse. They learn how to hide their pain and alienate themselves to avoid judgment."

My scarred skin itches beneath the spotlight behind me, and my voice quivers. "While these adaptations are coping mechanisms, they can be insidious and harmful. Abused women second-guess themselves so much they can lose themselves in a deep hole of self-hatred and hopelessness. They need a support system, friends, family, people who will inspire them to seek help. People who will support them through recovery."

For the next ten minutes, I walk through the signs of abuse, what to look for, and how domestic violence hotlines can help. When I finish the final bullet point, I sway at the podium, wrestling with indecision and the urge to throw up.

It would be so easy to end the speech now, wrap the shawl around my back, and return to Decker. He'll be disappointed, but he'll still choose me. Because he loves me.

What will you give up for this man?

I look out into the crowd, instantly transfixed by the adoration shining in his eyes. He's the best thing that ever happened to me, and there's still so much I want to do with him. I want to hold his hand in a movie theater, wear his underwear to bed, laugh with him until my stomach stitches, make out in a public restroom, and fall hopelessly in love with him every day for the rest of my life.

I want to sacrifice for him. I would give him everything, give up all of it, just to wake beside him every morning.

With a shaky hand, I remove the wireless microphone from the stand and step to the side of the podium. "It's easy to put on a ninety-thousand-dollar gown and strut through a fancy ballroom. But to expose your mistakes, to wear your imperfections for all to see? That takes strength." I pull in a deep breath. "Strength is a concept I've struggled with. What does it look like? Is it aggressive and ballsy? Does it have eight-pack abs?"

I aim a pointed look at Decker, and the crowd erupts in laughter. His expression remains neutral, intense.

"How is strength achieved?" I sweep my eyes through the room, trembling with nervous dread. "Can you grow strong through sheer force of will? I struggled with this concept because I haven't been strong in a long time. I've been hiding. Afraid. Terrified my weaknesses will show through my designer clothes." A flurry of emotion thickens my voice and burns through my sinuses. "I've recently learned I have the power to make myself feel strong and worthy."

I can do this. I can do this. I know I can.

"I was a victim of abuse. I was beaten, violated, and disfigured."

A ripple of energy stirs through the audience.

"The who, when, and how aren't important. If you ask, I won't disclose it. I'm not that victim anymore." Tears gather in my eyes, but I refuse to let them fall. "It took me a long time, but I see my strength now. I found it in the transition between hurting and healing, between hiding and surviving, between seeking acceptance and falling in love." I find Decker's eyes and imagine his raspy tone in my ear. "Sometimes you just need a shift in perspective, and everything on the outside will change with it. But more than that, you need the support from someone who cares." I stand taller. "I'm a survivor, and I see strength in my scars."

My heart pounds as I set the mic on the podium. The crowd explodes in applause, and my stomach hardens. I gulp down breaths, but the moment I meet Decker's eyes, the dread loosens from my muscles. He believes in me. He loves me. I can do this.

Picking up the fur wrap, I hug it to my mid-section. Then slowly, wobbly, I turn, giving the audience a direct view of my exposed back.

The applause fades to a few claps. Then a single wavering clap. Then nothing.

Silence. Lots of it.

They're in shock. Can't blame them. I told them I had scars. I didn't say twenty-six knife wounds.

The deafening hush continues, interrupted by the sound of a cough. The clink of utensils. Footsteps shuffling near the exit. Every little noise shivers goosebumps up my scarred spine. How long should I let them stare?

The tension-filled seconds feel like hours. Tremors ripple through my legs, threatening to knock me over. God, this is harder than I thought, but beneath the strangling fist of fear lurks a profound feeling. For the first time in six years, I feel liberated. Uninhibited by a mask. I finally feel free.

Turn around, Laynee. Turn around and face them.

Straightening my shoulders, I pivot toward the room.

Decker stands beside steps of the stage, hands clasped behind his back, and pride glowing on his face. My lungs fill with air, and a smile twitches my mouth.

I stride toward him, holding his gaze while raising my voice to the crowd. "Enjoy the rest of your meal. The auction will begin shortly."

When I reach the stairs, he offers his hand. I curl my fingers around his, and he leads me down the steps. Near our table, he pulls me against his chest, and the moment I smell his skin, I know I'm home. It's an earthy scent, natural and wild, like the air that breathes through my Savannah acreage. I press closer to him, savoring that nostalgic aroma.

Chatter and movement arises around us, but nothing can distract me from the scent of his skin, the palm resting on my cheek, and the soft kiss on my lips.

"I did it," I say into his mouth.

"I never doubted." He rests his forehead against mine and runs his hand up and down my bare spine. "I know I'm a horny bastard, but watching you up there made my slacks unbearably tight. We can leave now, right?"

I reverse out of his arms, shaking my head and grinning. "After the auction, I'm all yours."

With a groan, he takes my hand and weaves us around the crowded tables. My gaze skips from face to face, and every pair of eyes averts from mine. If I made these superficial prima donnas uncomfortable, so be it. I'll know soon enough who my friends are. No doubt news is already spreading outside this room. Good thing I didn't bring my phone tonight. Violet is probably leaving me hate mail at this very moment.

I spot Reese standing against the far wall, glaring at the screen of his phone with a pained look on his face. My stomach plunges, and I squeeze Decker's hand, veering us toward my best friend.

As we approach, Reese looks up, and a warm smile hijacks his lips.

"That was fucking amazing, Laynee." He pockets the phone and pulls me in for a hug.

"Thank you. What were you scowling at?" I step back. "Has it hit the news feeds yet?"

"It's still too early to gauge." He takes the shawl from my hand. "I'll go check this for you."

I watch him damn near sprint away with a sinking feeling in my gut. "It must be bad."

"Maybe. Maybe not." Decker brushes a ringlet of

hair away from my face. "But the woman who just gave a poignant speech on strength doesn't give a flying fuck about gossip."

I open my mouth to remind him that gossip can ruin my career, but I'm interrupted by the one person I'm anxious to see after my speech. "Mrs. Montague."

"Darling." She accepts my offered hand and holds it between us. "Let me just say I've always been impressed by your poise and gentility, but now I'm… Well, I'm happy *you* finally see your strength. Thank you for sharing it with us." She tightens her grip and releases my fingers. "You're an inspiration, Miss Somerset."

"Thank you." I press a hand to my chest, feeling lighter, *relieved.*

"Mr. Gabrielli?" She looks at Decker. "You'll be in touch?"

"Count on it." He winks.

"Wonderful." She lifts her chin. "I wish you both the best of luck."

With that, she glides through the ballroom and slips out the exit.

For the next hour, Decker and I watch the auction from a table in the corner of the ballroom. Other than Adelaide, no one approaches me or makes eye contact. I know I said not to ask questions about my scars, but I expected some kind of reaction—censure, pity, approval. *Something.*

A few forced smiles are thrown my way, but I have the distinct feeling I'm being snubbed. These people are nothing if not two-faced. I don't put it past them to pretend I don't exist then talk viciously behind my back. Most of them are entitled shallow snobs, more concerned about image and money than raising proceeds for an honorable cause. After all, it's out of concern for their public image that brings them here. The press coverage tonight is huge. What better way to make a positive public appearance than to be caught on camera at a charity event?

As the bids close out on each item in the auction, my suspicions progress into panic.

"The auction usually brings in more money than this." I grip Decker's hand on my thigh. "The bids are a fraction of what they've been in prior years."

"You know what I think?" He waits until I look at him before leaning in and baring his teeth. "Fuck. Them."

I liquefy in the chair, because dammit, the way he says *fuck,* all cocky and belligerent, turns me into butter.

"You, in a tux, should be censored." I tilt my head at the dwindling crowd, the majority of which is female. "I bet most of these socialites are only lingering with the hope to steal a few minutes alone with you."

"Now that you mention it, I've needed to take a piss for a while now." His sexy lips slant into an infectious smile.

"Are you babysitting me?"

"No, I'm staring at your hard nipples, waiting for them to poke through the fabric of your dress."

He has, in fact, paid a lot of attention to my chest tonight.

"Go to the bathroom, you ass." I give his jaw a playful shove and stand. "The auction's almost finished. I'm going to step out onto the veranda."

"I'll find you." He leaves me with a scorching kiss and prowls out of the ballroom.

Since I've only had two glasses of champagne tonight, I grab another from a passing waiter and wander toward the outside balcony. In prior years, the ballroom remained packed several hours after the auction. This year, the crowd has already thinned out so much I don't encounter a single person on my way to the French doors.

Apprehension sits heavy in my stomach. Did everyone leave because of me? Maybe it's arrogant to assume such a thing, but the attendees seem to be avoiding me like a plague. Are my scars really so hideous they make people uneasy? It's not like they're contagious.

As I reach the open doors to the veranda, a familiar voice stops me in my tracks.

"She's still whining." Blake huffs an empty laugh. "Seriously, I had to listen to that through two years of marriage. I couldn't get away from her pathetic sniveling fast enough."

The tips of my ears catch fire, and my teeth slam together. Sniveling? I never did that. I never said a goddamn word to him about my scars. I'm not without shortcomings, but whining isn't one of them.

I back up and press against the wall around the corner before Blake and his audience of five women sees me. My hand trembles so badly I put the full flute of champagne on the tray stand beside me.

"You have to tell us, Blake," one of the women says. "How did she get the scars?"

"She hid it from me, like some big dirty secret." His voice lowers. "I think she did it to herself. You know, like one of those cutters. She's messed up in the head."

The women on the patio burst into laughter, and I cover my mouth to stifle my horrified gasp. I can't stop the moisture from burning my eyes, and I hate myself for it. He doesn't have power over me anymore. I need to walk away and not react. I'm stronger than this.

"Can you believe that performance tonight?" Blake chuckles. "Flashing her old butchered body has got to be the most vulgar, look-at-me, attention-seeking stunts in the history of the movie business."

"Oh my God, Blake." A woman giggles. "You're terrible."

Blood cooks in my veins, and tears stream down my face. I did a good thing, the *right* thing. So why am I letting them make me feel so fucking rejected, humiliated, and *furious?*

"As if her age isn't problematic enough," another woman says. "I just feel sad for her. I mean, her career's over, you know?"

"Her career was over at thirty," Blake says. "Her desperation to impress is, as ever, exhausting to watch. And this thing tonight is downright repulsive. As old as she is, she should know better."

My ribs squeeze painfully, and a horrible ache consumes my chest. If I listen to much more, I'll end up giving them a real reason to mock me, because right now, I want nothing more than to run in there, punching, screaming, and clawing out eyeballs.

I move to leave and stop at the sound of footfalls racing across the veranda. A masculine grunt rents the air, followed by metal chair legs screeching across concrete, then the shrieking cries of the women.

What the hell? I turn back, round the corner, and stumble onto the patio.

Chairs are tossed over. The women huddle off to the side, and Blake is sprawled on the ground with Decker's forearm against his throat.

Adrenaline rushes through me, and my ankles

teeter in the heels as I move toward them. Decker locks Blake's back to his chest, and his arm hooks so tightly beneath Blake's chin, the skin around Blake's pinched features is turning blue.

"Decker." I crouch beside him. "He can't breathe."

"That's the fucking point." His eyes are darker than I've ever seen, full of so much rage and brutal intent.

He must've come out here through the side doors. I don't know how much of the conversation he heard, but it was enough to redden his complexion, turn his jaw to stone, and put a terrifyingly deadly look on his face.

Blake flops and kicks in Decker's stranglehold, wrinkling his expensive tux and dragging his shiny shoes over the concrete. His fingers work frantically to pry the arm off his throat, but he won't be going anywhere unless Decker allows it.

Pulse racing, I clutch Decker's flexed bicep and dig my nails in. "Give him air."

Decker grunts a deep, angry noise and loosens his hold just enough for Blake to gasp.

A squeak draws my attention to the huddled women. Fuck, they're going to have a field day with the press over this.

"Everyone out. Now!" I cast them an infuriated glare, and thankfully, they hurry away. I turn back to Decker. "Let him go."

"That's fucking bullshit, Laynee. You don't know how badly I want to break his fucking face. I want to break every bone in his body. He's a waste of goddamn space."

Now that Blake can breathe, he takes the

opportunity to laugh hoarsely. "You're letting this guy stick his dick in you? You're old enough to be his mother."

In a blur of limbs, Decker flips Blake beneath him and straddles the other man's hips, putting himself in the most dominant Jiu-Jitsu position. He's effectively pinned Blake to the ground, face up, so he can pound the ever-loving shit out of every vulnerable body part.

"Decker, don't." I touch his shoulder and holy fuck, he's tense. I harden my tone. "If he walks out of here bloody—"

"He won't be able to walk."

"—tomorrow's headlines will read *Laynee Somerset's anti-violence charity dinner ends in a violent crime of passion. As it turns out, she's not over Blake Harridan.* Please, think through this. You'll undo every right and good thing we've done here tonight."

Decker's chest heaves, and the tendons in his neck strain against his skin. After an endless moment, he closes his eyes. When he opens them, he shoves off Blake and grabs my hand. "Let's go."

I hurry to keep up with his long-legged strides, but we only make it a couple steps before Blake opens his idiot mouth.

"You always were a weak little bitch, Laynee."

Decker slams to a halt.

"He's baiting us." I tug him forward until Blake speaks again.

"I stretched out her cunt for you." He laughs. "But I wasn't able to iron out the wrinkles."

Fuck this. I whirl toward Blake, but Decker's already moving with murder in his eyes. I catch his arm.

"Let me." I don't wait for his response and

instead walk up to my grinning ex-husband.

Rearing back my fist, I swing toward his face. As expected, he dodges, laughing, and I slam my knee into his groin—the same way I did to Decker yesterday. Only this time, I hit harder, pouring all my strength into it, ruthlessly fueled by righteous anger.

I step back as he doubles over. Decker moves in and rains punch after punch on Blake's torso. Blake moans and swings his arms, but Decker's a skilled fighter. Blake doesn't stand a chance of landing a single strike.

Glancing at the exits, I confirm no one's watching. Then I turn back to appreciate the solid mass of muscle bunching and contracting beneath Decker's tux. His strikes are so vicious they knock Blake off his feet. Decker doesn't let up, and I don't interfere. Whatever comes out of this, it's worth the deep satisfaction of watching my ex-husband finally get what was coming to him.

Decker doesn't once hit Blake's face, and there isn't a drop of visible blood. When Blake starts to cry beneath the hammering hits, Decker grabs his throat and leans in.

"If you mention to anyone that I so much as touched you, Laynee will release all the evidence she has against you."

Blake's pink eyes widen and dart to me.

I don't have any evidence of Blake's abuse, but I roll with it. "I hid cameras in our house, Blake. I have hours of footage."

He drops his head back on the concrete and groans. "Fuck."

"Let's go home, baby." Decker hooks an arm around my back and guides me to the door.

A few minutes later, I walk out of the event with my shoulders back, chin high, and the scarred lines of my back on full display. And just like he vowed, Decker's right there beside me.

On the way home, he makes me promise not to turn on my phone or look at the news until tomorrow. Given how quickly the event cleared out and Reese's unusual silence as he steals peeks at his phone, I assume the worst. But I'm on board with Decker's demand. Doesn't matter what we do tonight, the shit storm will still be waiting for us tomorrow.

The moment we step inside the house, his deep timbre infiltrates my senses. "I want those gorgeous lips wrapped around my cock."

"Is that right?" I saunter backwards, twirling a finger in the loose curl dangling beside my face.

"You think I'm playing?" He prowls after me, his expression searing and dead serious. "I'm about two seconds from fucking your face."

I gulp as each beat of my heart descends lower, lower, until the only beat I feel is the heavy, hard pulse between my legs.

He catches me at the bottom of the stairs and slides a hand around my throat. Adept fingers quickly loosen the tie at my neck and lower the front of the dress to my waist. He follows the fall of satin with scorching wet kisses. With my chest and back bare, he doesn't waste time stripping my lower body.

My gown and panties pool around my feet, and a draft from a nearby vent blows a shiver across my skin.

In the span of a languid blink, the space between us melts away. His hands stab through my hair, plucking out pins until the curls fall around my shoulders. His lips capture mine, and his tongue dips in, licking the inside of my mouth with wicked deep thrusts.

I circle my arms around his waist and palm his ass through the slacks, molding my fingers against the hard muscles that tighten with the rock of his hips. His swollen length jabs against my stomach, and my tight nipples drag across the material of his tux, heightening the pleasure. A rapture of sensation swamps my insides, stirring a need that only this man can quench.

"Take me out." His voice is broken glass, smooth and hard with cutting edges.

With him fully dressed in his sexy tuxedo, I remove his cock and suck it until his thighs shake, his head falls back, and his come shoots down my throat. He returns the favor by spreading me out on the stairs and burying his face between my legs.

We fuck against the wall, on the couch, and on the landing upstairs. When we finally make it to the bedroom, we lie naked on the bed, chest to chest, absorbed in our bubble and kissing without urgency. Our mouths are exploratory and giving and vibrating with passion. When he fucks me again, it doesn't feel like fucking. It feels like love.

We remain entwined for hours, our bodies joined in the most intimate way, savoring every second as if it's our last in this world.

As it turns out, it's our last reprieve for a long time.

Chapter 23

Decker

It's all unraveling. *We* are unraveling.

I pace through the kitchen, one hand squeezing my phone, the other pulling angrily at my uncombed hair.

"Rein it in, man." Reese sits at the island and pulls a long draw from his beer. "This is just a bump in the road."

"You call this a bump?" I whirl on him and stab a finger toward the ceiling. "She hasn't left the bedroom in a week!"

The charity dinner brought in a fraction of the donations it yielded in prior years. Tweeters are calling her reveal a wardrobe malfunction, and public attention has propagated the hatred. The barrage of comments on-line has been so overwhelmingly cruel and unsupportive I can't eat or sleep. The guilt is unbearable.

"I did this to her." Pain sears through my chest. "I forced this decision upon her." *What have I done?*

"What you did was show her how strong and beautiful she is. You *empowered* her." Reese sighs. "She knew what the ramifications would be. Give her a little credit, Decker. When this eventually blows over, she won't regret it."

"Will it blow over?" *Have I ruined her career?*

He takes another gulp of beer and stares out the kitchen window. "I don't know."

My heart sinks beneath the gravity of the situation. She has enough money to retire from the limelight, but that's not what I want for her. Because that's not what *she* wants. She worked too goddamn hard to spend the rest of her life hiding from the glare of publicity.

I've been tethered to my phone for the past week, obsessing over every post and article. I lived in a naive world before this. A world where I thought the best of people. I was wrong. So fucking wrong.

Giving into the compulsion to read the latest updates on my notification alerts, I stare at the screen of my phone with the hope that the consensus has finally shifted.

Laynee Somerset must've slept on a hand grenade. Her back is hell on earth. Wish she would've kept that horror show to herself. #sharingisnotcaring #gross

Move over muffin tops and beer guts. Laynee Somerset coming in as the star of scars.

Who stabbed Laynee Somerset? I heard it's just a publicity stunt. Conspiracy theorists want to know.

People are saying @layneesomerset is hideous?! Well if that's hideous I'd like some of that please. She looks amazing.

No wonder the gorgeous Blake Harridan cheated on her #beautyandthescarredbeast #epicromancefail

Am I the only one turned off by Laynee's pity party? Lil too much too late IMO

Edgy and twitchy, I shut off the screen and toss the phone on the counter. I want to respond to every single one of those body-shaming motherfuckers. I want to fucking annihilate them. How can they think of her as anything less than perfect? Killer body, exquisite face, with a personality and strength of character that's incomparable. She's the whole package. What the hell is wrong with people?

The day after the event, she posted a message that was inspirational and uplifting, reminding the world what it means to be confident in your skin. But the rally of her supporters continues to be overshadowed by spineless criticism.

The only good news is Blake has kept his fat fucking mouth shut about our confrontation. If he changes his mind, I'm more than ready to pay him a visit.

"You need to stop reading that shit." Reese stands to toss his beer in the trash and grab another one. "There will always be haters. The professional drama-feeders, attention whores, unhappy souls who hide behind their anonymity and bash everyone they envy. None of those dickheads would have the balls to say something to her face. She knows this, because unfortunately, this isn't her first rodeo."

"Then why is she taking it so hard?" I've never seen her so despondent. *Defeated.* It's fucking wrecking me. "I've tried talking to her. I've tried patience. You and I both know she doesn't respond to either."

He shrugs and stares down at his beer, his eyes shuttering.

"What?" I get in his face. "What are you not saying?"

"I don't know, Decker. When I brought her home six years ago, after she spent hours on that operating table fighting for her life, she shut everyone out. Honestly, she didn't really have people in her life anyway. Her parents were dead. Her friends were phony and untrustworthy. All she had was a bi-sexual assistant, who was too young to know what to say or how to respond to her trauma. I did my best to be there for her, but she was alone. No one knew what had happened to her. In a way, that was a blessing, because she didn't have to prove anything to anyone except herself. She took her time nursing her wounds. She wasn't pressured to bounce back in record time. In the end, she did bounce back."

"What are you saying?" I lower onto the stool beside him. "You think I'm pressuring her? She doesn't have to prove shit to me."

"I think she's…uncertain. Your relationship is new and fragile, and you already know her history with men. She's batting zero for three, if you count me."

"But her relationship with me is—"

"Bound by an agreement. *You* might've forgotten that you're being paid to be here, but I guarantee she's thinking about that now. She made a huge fucking sacrifice for you."

I inhale sharply. "I wanted her to do it for herself."

"Doesn't matter. She did it for you. She didn't want you to be disappointed, and I imagine right now, with the negative reactions to her scars, she's feeling like a disappointment. You wanted the world to embrace her, and she didn't make that happen."

"Fuck them. I don't give a fuck what they think."

"Then why did you want her to expose her vulnerability to them?"

"Because I'm an idiot."

"You're not just an idiot." He grips my neck and gives it a hard squeeze. "You're an idiot in love."

I can't argue that. "What do you suggest I do?"

"Let Violet do what she does. She'll fix this, and

by *fix this* I mean she'll spin the story the way it should've been received. In the meantime, take care of our girl. Prove to her you're not going anywhere."

"I've told her over and over—"

"Trey and Blake told her the same thing. *Prove* it."

I lower my head in my hands, clenching my fingers in my hair. "How?"

"I don't have a clue."

"And here I thought all your words of wisdom were actually leading to tangible advice."

"Guess that's why I'm still single." He flashes his megawatt smile.

Single is not a status I ever want to hold again, and for the next two weeks, I make damn sure Laynee knows it.

Her publicist smooths over the negative press by redirecting the focus to raising awareness for victims of abuse. I don't know how Violet does it, but she wrangles the support from the most authoritative sources on celebrity news. When the media buzz finally fades, it ends on message of survival. Laynee's not willing to share her story publicly, but she wears—and will continue to wear—her scars openly as a symbol of strength.

Like her, her public image will forever be scarred. There will always be those who can't look past her skin. Nevertheless, she throws herself back into work, including our morning runs and nightly spar sessions. But there's something straining between us, a crack in the foundation of our relationship. I can't pinpoint it exactly. Physically, nothing's changed. But emotionally, she seems withdrawn, cautious, unsure.

I continue to leave notes in random places for her to find, prepare all her favorite foods, and kiss her endlessly like the lovesick fool that I am. What I don't do is say those three significant words.

The words are there, hovering on my lips every second of every day. But the timing is wrong. I don't want her to mistake my declaration as an expression of pity or desperation. When I tell her I love her, it will be backed up by a gesture that can't be misconstrued.

The gesture doesn't come to me until one of my late-night laps in the pool. Laynee was on the phone all day with her agent and went to bed early. Distracted and restless, I work out my energy in the crystal blue water, thinking about the moment I initiated the conversation about our future.

Where do you see us at the end of this agreement?

We said a lot of things that day, but my biggest take away was the question she asked herself.

What will you give up for this man?

She's more than proven her love for me. What grand gesture have I made? What have I sacrificed?

I swim to the stairs and sit on the top step, catching my breath beneath the ethereal glow of the moon. I live in her beautiful home, eat her food, and wear the clothes purchased with her money. And I'm in the process of launching the most important business venture of my life with the financial support and affluence of *her* friend.

I haven't made a single sacrifice. Contrarily, every aspect of my world has spectacularly improved. Because of her.

What will I give up for her? The answer is everything. All of it. Yet she's asked for nothing.

Only that's not true. There's one thing. She asked for one impossible, stomach-curling thing, and I outright refused.

I lie back on the concrete, every muscle in my body tensing at the thought. And that's when I finally understand the crushing depths of sacrifice.

I know what I need to do.

CHAPTER 24

Laynee

I brace my hands against the tiles of the shower wall as warm water rains over my head. In the month following the charity dinner, I've gone through a parade of emotions. Regret, self-pity, rage, love, and deep despair. But most of all, I've felt like a failure. A failure to myself, to all the victims of abuse, and to Decker.

He had such high hopes for how my reveal would turn out, and his fury over the ugly reactions was devastating to witness. I know he was angry *for me*, not at me. He's been nothing but protective and kind. But I can't help feeling like an epic disappointment.

When I'm alone, I let myself wallow and doubt. Am I enough for him? Does he truly love me? Will he stay when he's no longer paid to do so? I hate the doubt. It's unproductive and self-destructive, but I'm only human, as much as the rest of the world likes to forget that.

Decker doesn't forget. He's always in my face, pressing me to talk, to share, to not pull away. I fucking love him for that. I love him so much it hurts.

I turn off the water and stare at my pruney fingers. Jesus, I must've been in here for an hour. I need to stop this. Stop hiding from him. Stop protecting myself from the possibility of heartache. Because it's too late for that. If he leaves me, there will be no escape from the pain.

He isn't Trey or Blake or even Reese. Decker is it for me, and I'll fight for him until the last breath in my body.

I step out of the shower and wrap a towel around me. Steam hovers in the room as I run a brush through my hair and moisturize my face, opting to skip my whole nightly facial routine. All I want to do right now is go snuggle up to the sexy man who occupies my every thought.

When I enter the bedroom, the first thing I notice is the armchair sitting near the foot of the bed. Decker must've moved it from the corner of the room. Why?

He steps through the doorway, but he's not alone. Reese trails behind him, and they both look guilty of something.

"What are you two up to?" I tighten the towel around me, surprised Decker isn't losing his shit because I'm wearing next to nothing in front of Reese.

Decker strides toward the foot of the bed and pats the mattress. "Sit."

"Okay." I obey with a belly full of nerves. I don't know what to make of his gruff tone and severe expression. "What's this about?"

He moves to stand in front of the armchair, which is five feet away and facing the bed. Looks like he set up a confrontational sit down, like an intervention or something. Is that why Reese is here? But an intervention for what? I'm really confused.

Clasping his hands behind him, Decker widens his stance, filling my view with his strong muscular physique. The Eminem t-shirt molds to his ripped pecs and washboard abs. Biceps curve away from wide shoulders. Denim stretches around long defined legs, and the low dip of the waistband reveals indentations of V-cut that I love to trace with my tongue.

When I lift my gaze, the smoldering look in his eyes chases away my apprehension and arouses the feminine parts of me that will forever be obsessively and completely in love with this man.

"You've only ever asked me for one thing." His gravelly voice flows through me in shivery waves. "You should know I'll give you anything, baby. Anything at all."

What did I ask him for? I rack my distracted brain and shake my head, staring up at him. "Decker, I don't—"

"Reese." He gives my best friend a chin lift.

Reese reaches behind his head and pulls off his t-shirt, exposing his lean runner's build. He's a gorgeous man, but he isn't Decker. And why is he taking off his shirt? Decker does the same, and now I'm staring at two shirtless men in my bedroom.

I glance down at my tiny towel. "I'm suddenly feeling overdressed. You guys better start talking."

"We're not here to talk." Decker's pecs twitch and something akin to nervousness flashes across his expression.

Realization dawns a second before Reese steps in front of Decker and lowers to his knees, putting him eye-level with Decker's groin.

You and Reese. I want to watch him suck your cock.

My eyes widen, and my heart rate explodes. "Oh my God." I breathe in, out, unable to control my gasps. "You can't be serious. I mean, you don't want this, and I won't—"

Reese groans. "Shut up, Laynee." His hands fly to

Decker's waist, and his fingers dig in.

"No talking, Reese." Decker fists a hand in Reese's blond hair, and that hard grip sends a tremor down Reese's spine.

"But your friendship." I rub a hand over my face. Am I really trying to talk him out of this? "It'll make things weird and…I don't know…really fucking awkward."

"Reese and I discussed this like grown responsible men."

Reese laughs.

Decker pulls tighter on his hair, silencing him. "He's here willingly."

"Sorry, Laynee." Reese adjusts his fingers on Decker's waist. "I've been trying to get into your boyfriend's pants for six months."

I slap a hand over the grin controlling my lips.

"He's full of shit." Decker slowly releases a breath. "Here's how this is going to go. You will remove the towel. Reese is going to keep his eyes on me at all times. After you spread your legs, you're going to play with your tight little pussy. Neither of you will come until I give you permission."

Wet heat rushes between my legs, and I moan.

"You're already soaked, aren't you?"

I glance at the back of Reese's head and nod.

"Show me." Decker's growly demand drowns my senses in desire.

Shucking the towel to the floor, I widen my legs and place my feet on the edge of the mattress. He's seen every bare inch of me countless times, but this feels different, more vulnerable. Maybe because I'm so spread out and he's staring, like really staring. Hard.

"Christ, I never tire of looking at you." His

nostrils flare with a deep breath. "One more thing, baby. Reese is here to fulfill your fantasy and no doubt one of his own."

Reese makes a groaning noise in his throat.

"He's *not* here to be a buffer between us," Decker says firmly. "I know that's how you two used to operate."

"I don't need a buffer with you. I don't want one. Ever."

His shoulders loosen. "If I could break the one-year agreement, I would. I don't want to be paid to be with you, Laynee." He scratches his whiskered cheek, studying my face. "I called Karen at Infidelity and told her I won't be renewing my employment with them at the end of the year. I intend to buy out the agreement."

My pulse quickens. Renewing the agreement would've given him another year's salary. Buying it out means he intends to stay with me without Infidelity or the income.

I'll buy out the contract, but we can argue about that later.

"I'm doing this," he says, glancing down at Reese and returning to me, "to prove I will do *anything* for you. Not for money. Not for career opportunities. Not for sexual gratification. I'm doing this simply because it makes you happy."

The golden-brown of his irises holds me for an exposed, vulnerable instant as the depth of his love swallows the space between us. He's offering such an inconceivably selfless gift, and I'm overcome with gratitude, solidarity, and bone-deep peace.

"You don't have to do this." I hold his gaze. "If you're not sure…"

"I'm sure of you. *Us.*"

A ray of warmth bursts through my chest.

Decker releases Reese's hair and pats his cheek. "Go ahead."

Oh my God. This is really happening.

Reese slides his hands to the front of Decker's jeans. The button pulls through. The zipper sounds its seductive crawl downward. My fingers move of their own volition, tracing the wet flesh around my opening.

Six months ago, Reese tried to suck Decker's cock. It ended with him in a chokehold and me trying to break the Infidelity agreement. We've come so far, and we'll continue to progress with or without this grand gesture. Which is why my stomach cramps with fear. Should I let this continue? Will he begrudge me after? Will he forgive me if I put the brakes on something he's trying to gift me?

Reese shifts Decker's jeans down his hips, revealing a huge *soft* cock.

He isn't aroused. He doesn't want this.

"Decker, this is wrong." I close my legs and wrap my arms around my torso. "I feel really selfish. I can't let you—"

"Shut the fuck up and put your fingers in your pussy." He lowers into the chair. "Spread yourself open so I can see you."

I follow his order, fingers tentative as I touch myself. I start to slip into my flustered mind, but the heat in his eyes holds me in the room, in the moment, with him. Those eyes wander down my chest, making my breasts feel fuller, heavier. His gaze roams lower, tracing the spread of my legs and following the movement of my hand as I sink my fingers deeper inside my pussy.

"You're a vision, Laynee. A fucking dream. Don't

stop touching yourself." He rakes a hand through Reese's hair and yanks on the strands. "Reese, pull out your cock."

Reese drags in a shaky breath and fumbles with his belt, then his zipper. His jeans inch down his backside, exposing the upper curves of his ass. I can't see the front of him, but the flex of his bicep and the movement of his arm tells me he's stroking himself. My God, it's so fucking hot.

I've done things like this with Reese, but we've never had anyone commanding us, divvying out the pleasure, and controlling the outcome. I don't know why it's so arousing to be dominated by Decker, but it makes all the difference in the world.

Reese continues to stroke himself, working his body into a breathy, muscle-strained mass of tension. "Decker?"

Beyond Reese's shoulders, Decker's length twitches, swells, and lengthens. There's nothing more erotic than watching Decker get hard.

His eyes don't stray from mine as he curls his fingers around the armrests. "Suck my cock, Reese."

Air whooshes from my lungs, and I rub myself harder, more frantically. I'm already climbing toward climax, but I don't slow down. I can't.

Inching to the side, Reese deliberately gives me a direct view of his free hand wrapping around Decker's erection. The instant Reese grips him, Decker chokes on a breath, and every muscle in his body goes stiff.

I spread my thighs wider, sliding my fingers in and out without breaking eye contact with Decker. But when he sucks in a harsh inhale, I can't stop myself from watching his cock sink into Reese's mouth.

Oh.

My.

Fuck.

Decker grunts and shifts his legs, planting his bare feet firmly to the floor.

My focus flits to the white-knuckled grip of Decker's hands on the chair. The corded sinews in his neck. The rapid rise and fall of his sculpted chest. The glorious play of muscles flexing in his torso. The blown pupils eclipsing the brown of his eyes.

When his chest goes still, I'm not sure he's breathing. But he's watching. Watching my fingers with resolute focus.

The brawn of Reese's back trembles beneath a sheen of perspiration as he bobs his head and slides his hand over his own cock. My breaths wheeze with growing urgency, threading through the sounds of masculine grunts. Decker looks so tense and stunned I don't know if he's going to explode with pleasure or rage.

He seems to lose some kind of fight with his lungs, because he releases a heavy loud exhale, and the fire in his eyes intensifies. "You need to come, Laynee. Come now."

I circle a finger around my clit, and a release of tingling electricity detonates in my core, shooting outward like fireworks, crackling, sparking, zapping every nerve ending in my body. My head drops back, and I continue to rub, moaning and jerking beneath my fingers.

Reese moans with me, his voice garbled and pained. I return my attention to them just as Decker grips Reese's hair and pulls, freeing his cock from Reese's mouth.

"Come," he mutters, holding my gaze.

Reese's arm jerks, once, two more times, and he groans long and hard, dropping his forehead to Decker's thigh, his entire body shaking with the force of his release. Decker strokes Reese's hair through the orgasm and continues to do so while Reese catches his breath, all the while staring directly into my eyes.

"Fuck." Reese chuckles and grabs his t-shirt, using it to clean himself.

As he fastens his jeans, Decker cups a hand against Reese's jaw, and they share a moment of eye contact. I can't see Reese's face, but Decker's gaze softens, as if to silently say, *Thank you*. Then Decker smirks and gives him a pat on his head.

An unexpected tremble of relief sifts through me.

Climbing to his feet, Reese leans over to whisper something in Decker's ear. The skin around Decker's eyes creases, and he gives a stiff nod.

"See you tomorrow, Laynee." Reese strolls to the door, keeping his gaze averted from my nude body.

"Okay." I wait until the door closes behind him before pointing out the obvious. "You didn't come."

"I only come in *you*."

My chest tightens. In a really good way. "What did he say to you?"

A smile twitches his lips, and he rubs it away. "He told me not to fuck this up."

"There's no way you could—"

"I love you." He stands and removes his jeans and briefs. "I've loved you for months." He stalks toward me, eyes full of conviction and promise.

My heart swells with aching joy, and my eyes prick with tears. I scoot backward, inching toward the headboard, lost in his gaze.

"I love you in this moment." He crawls onto the

mattress, chasing me with calculated slowness. "I'll love you in every moment that follows, every month, every year, for a million light years."

"That's a long time."

"It won't be long enough." He grips my ankle and yanks me beneath him, staring at me for a span of several heartbeats. "I can't believe you're mine."

My face crumples as I fight back tears. "Stop making me cry and fuck me."

He bares his teeth in a predatory smile and slams his mouth against mine. Tongues collide, fingers entwine, and soul meets soul. He's a feeling I've never felt. An emotion without limits. An agreement that doesn't expire. He's the only place I want to be.

I breathe in his scent—the earthy, elemental aroma of home and him. He rests his palm on my cheek and kisses me until I'm breathless, mindless, and insane with need.

He's so hot and hard between my legs, and I'm soaked from the inside out. So when he finally presses against me, my body sucks him in, and we both groan.

"I love you," I breathe against his lips.

"I know." He thrusts and doesn't waste time setting a pace that crashes the headboard against the wall.

I scream his name as he plows me into the mattress. I whisper his name between toe-curling kisses. His name rides on my breaths as I surrender to him, arch beneath him, and follow him into a grunting, panting, body-trembling orgasm.

Sated and listless, we lie in a tangle of sweaty limbs and thumping heartbeats. We're so intertwined I don't know where I end and he begins. It makes me smile a smile I feel everywhere, and I press that smile against the warm skin of his neck, sharing it with him.

"You let Reese suck your cock." My smile widens.

"I've found I have no limits with you."

I lean up, sobering as I meet his eyes. "I won't abuse that."

"I know." His thumb traces the curve of my mouth.

"I mean it, Decker. It was selfish of me to demand that of you when I met you. I will *never* do that again."

His lashes sink half-mast. "Come here." He guides my face back to his neck.

I curl up against his chest and wrap my legs around his. "I want to do something for you. Anything. What do you need?"

"Eat. Sleep. Love my girl. Repeat." He strokes a hand through my hair. "That's all I need."

CHAPTER 25

Laynee

Six months later.

Sometimes it's easy to forget how I became Decker Gabrielli's girlfriend.

A profile with expectations and limits.

A binding legal agreement.

An exclusive company called Infidelity.

It all began one year ago today, which is why I'm on the phone with Karen Flores, sitting in the car with my driver instead of heading inside where I want to be. *With my boyfriend.*

"I was right." Barely restrained smugness teases through Karen's voice.

"I bet you love saying that."

"I say it a lot, but you didn't believe me."

"What do you want?" I sigh into the phone. "An apology?"

"If my memory's correct, you called me a bitch."

I cringe. Yeah, I might've used that word the night I tried to break the agreement.

"I'm sorry. I should've never gone off on you like that. You were right, and I was wrong. Really, really wrong." My tone is sincere, because I feel like a huge asshole. "He's everything, Karen. You couldn't have chosen a better man for me. *I* couldn't have chosen a better man. So I'm asking you to accept my apology and allow me to buy out the agreement. Pretty please with dollar signs on top."

"Consider it done. I'll forward the final paperwork to Reese Cromwell."

"Thank you." A feeling of weightlessness settles through me. "Thank you for everything. You changed my life."

"Glad to hear it, Miss Somerset. You're welcome."

I end the call and toss my phone in my bag. "I'm ready."

Rachel shifts in the driver seat and peers back at me. "Sure you don't want to go through the back door?"

I lean against the window and spot a dozen men and women near the front door of the building, holding markers, glossy photos, movie posters, and other memorabilia. "They look harmless. I'll be fine."

Brushing a hand through my hair, I don't look down at my workout clothes, which consists of a revealing sports bra and spandex shorts. I'm still not used to baring my scars in public, but day by day, it's getting easier.

I step out onto the curb of one of the busiest streets in downtown Savannah and head toward my destination two blocks away. Hanging above the door where my fans gather is a huge sign in yellow and turquoise letters.

Fight4U

I grin at the memory of the day it was hung. Decker was so happy he looked like his face would break from smiling. He didn't just open a self-defense school. He opened a nonprofit self-defense school for women. *Fight4U* runs on donations only. In fact, it started with an eye-watering donation made by Mrs. Adelaide Montague Fitzgerald.

He pays himself a measly salary, one he swears he can support us on should my career go to shit and I lose all my money. I wish he'd get his need to provide for me out of his head, but his male ego can be very narrow-minded. I love him for it.

When I reach the door, I pose for selfies and sign whatever is shoved in front of me.

"Thank you so much." A teenage girl snaps a photo with me, grinning from ear to ear. "I'm so excited you're going to Broadway. I'm already saving up so I can fly to New York to see your show."

"Thank you." I smile with her, sharing her excitement.

Stage acting is what separates the women from the girls. It's one thing to stand around a studio doing take after take until I get the scene right. But to stay in character for two hours amid the best of the best in Broadway talent? It's a scary, thrilling new adventure in my life. I'm ready to prove myself as an actress and add some hard-earned stage credits under my belt.

It also means Decker and I will be spending a lot of time in Manhattan. His Infidelity sponsor, Dr. Evan Daniels, was all too willing to give up his identity to host *Laynee Somerset* at his home during our visits. I met him and his boyfriend last month and felt at ease with them instantly. Evan is so blissfully happy and in love it glows on his face. I imagine that same look shines in my own eyes.

Twenty minutes later, the small crowd thins out. I catch Rachel out of the corner of my eye, where she watches over me a few feet away. She trains with Decker every week, as does the rest of my security team. I'd offer for her to join me now, but this is *my* time with him, and I'm extremely possessive of it.

He rents a small space of prime property in Savannah. A single room with no foyer. So when I slip inside, I do so quietly to avoid interrupting his class. I arrived early, hoping to watch him in action. But I lost time outside, and it looks like he's just wrapping up.

Standing in front of an audience of twenty or so women, he recaps the session and assigns homework.

Workout shorts hang low on his hips. His sculpted pecs and biceps are so pumped up the spandex shirt looks painted on. Every ripple and dip in his torso can be traced by the eye. No wonder his class hasn't noticed me leaning against the door. It's impossible to look away from him.

When he opened the school a couple months ago, he said he'd bring in a lot of students simply because he's Laynee Somerset's boyfriend. But his association with me has nothing to do with the popularity of his classes. They're here for him. He's sexy as fuck and one helluva instructor. Every woman in this room will finish his tutelage with a wealth of skill and confidence.

"That's all I have for you today." His eyes shift unerringly to mine, and his lips part in a smile he reserves just for me.

One by one, the women turn their heads, following his gaze, and the room erupts in gasps and squeals.

I spend another twenty minutes standing in for more photos and signing random things, including body parts. Then, finally, I have him alone.

He locks the front door and strips off his shirt. "I missed you."

We've only been separated for a couple hours,

but… "I missed you more."

After a few warm-up stretches, we circle each other on the mat.

"You're officially mine." I flex my fingers and roll my shoulders.

"I've always been yours. Are you wearing panties under those shorts?"

"No. I bought out the Infidelity agreement. We're no longer legally bound to stay together."

"Guess I'll have to bind you to me in other ways." He wings up a dark brow.

I narrow my eyes. "If that's a proposal—"

He attacks. My feet lose purchase with the floor, and in the next breath, I'm pinned beneath his heavy-ass body.

"When I propose," he breathes against my neck, "I'll knock you off your feet without touching you."

"Oh, well, that's only if I say *yes*."

He captures my mouth with his and kisses me until I forget what we were talking about.

Too soon, he leans back. "I sealed the deal with the Justice for Women Project."

"No shit?" My heart skips, and I hook my arms and legs around him in a full-body hug. "You really did?"

"I did."

The deal gives his school a wider reach. He raises money for Justice for Women, and they refer victims of abuse to him as part of their recovery. It's a huge win-win for all parties involved, and he pulled it off in a matter of months.

I stare up at him, awe-struck. "Look at you, getting ahead in the world. What's your secret?"

"You."

"No way. I don't get credit for any of this."

"You inspire me." He brushes an errant strand of hair from my face. "You inspired me to start a school for women. You inspire me to dream dreams. You inspire me to chase you until the end of time. You sweeten every effort and make every misstep an incentive to work harder."

My chest fills with a soul-deep breath. "Decker…"

"I live for you, Laynee. For your smile." He kisses my mouth. "For your body." He nuzzles my cleavage.

I laugh, squirming beneath his nipping teeth. "You live for rigorous, mutually-pleasurable, savage sex."

"With *you*." He touches his forehead to mine. "You, among all, will always be my favorite incentive."

OTHER BOOKS BY PAM GODWIN

LOVE TRIANGLE ROMANCE
TANGLED LIES TRILOGY
One is a Promise
Two is a Lie
Three is a War

DARK ROMANCE
DELIVER SERIES
Deliver #1
Vanquish #2
Disclaim #3
Devastate #4
Take #5
Manipulate #6
Unshackle #7
Dominate #8
Complicate #9

DARK COWBOY ROMANCE
TRAILS OF SIN
Knotted #1
Buckled #2
Booted #3

DARK ALASKAN ROMANCE

FROZEN FATE

Hills of Shivers and Shadows #1

Cage of Ice and Echoes #2

Heart of Frost and Scars #3

DARK PARANORMAL ROMANCE

TRILOGY OF EVE

Heart of Eve

Dead of Eve #1

Blood of Eve #2

Dawn of Eve #3

STUDENT-TEACHER / PRIEST

Lessons In Sin

STUDENT-TEACHER ROMANCE

Dark Notes

ROCK-STAR DARK ROMANCE

Beneath the Burn

BILLIONAIRE REVENGE

Dirty Ties

DARK HISTORICAL PIRATE ROMANCE

King of Libertines

Sea of Ruin

PAM GODWIN

New York Times, Wall Street Journal, and USA Today bestselling author, Pam Godwin, lives in the Midwest with her husband, cats, retired greyhounds, and an old, foul-mouthed parrot. She traveled the world for seven years, attended three universities, married the vocalist of her favorite rock band, and retired from her quantitative analyst career in 2014 to write full-time.

Her interests veer toward the unconventional: bourbon, full-body tattoos, and tragic villains. Equally peculiar are her aversions to sleeping, eating meat, and dolls with blinking eyes.

EMAIL: pamgodwinauthor@gmail.com

www.ingramcontent.com/pod-product-compliance
Lightning Source LLC
Chambersburg PA
CBHW020500310726
48979CB00016B/2736/J
9781966537151